CURVES IN THE ROAD

For information, contact the publisher, Hot Tree Publishing.
www.hottreepublishing.com
Editing: Hot Tree Editing
Cover Designer: Claire Smith
Interior Deisgner: RMGraphX
ISBN-10: 1-925448-82-7
ISBN-13: 978-1-925448-82-5
Second Edition
10 9 8 7 6 5 4 3 2

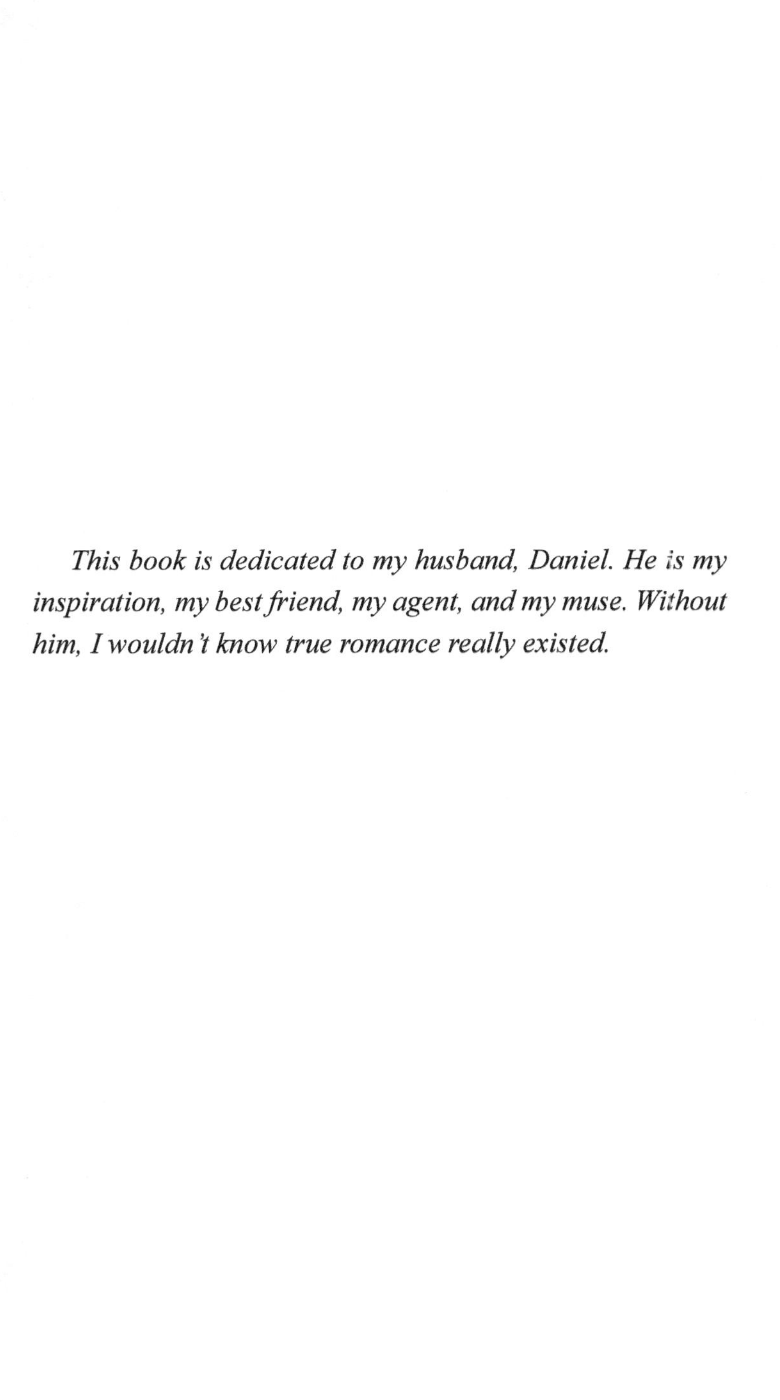

This book is dedicated to my husband, Daniel. He is my inspiration, my best friend, my agent, and my muse. Without him, I wouldn't know true romance really existed.

Prologue

When you build a road from one place to another, it won't always be a straight line. Sometimes you have to add curves to move around the natural obstacles. Life is like that as well. Sometimes we have a straight path to what we want in life, and we do everything possible to follow that path until suddenly a mountain appears, and we have to veer off course to get around it. Even though we face those curves, it doesn't mean we won't end up on the same path we started. Then again, sometimes we discover roads we never knew existed, and they will get us to where we want to be.

No matter how many curves you face, you inevitably end up where you were meant to be. It's a funny thing about fate; we try to control it, but no one can.

CHAPTER ONE

DERRICK

My four-year-old daughter, Katelyn, whimpered the entire way to the park, saying she didn't want to stay with a stranger. I breathed through my anxiety at leaving her. I hated the idea, but I had to get to the hospital. I didn't want Katelyn there. I had no real idea what shape my brother was in, and I wasn't willing to risk my daughter seeing her uncle injured.

She was always my priority. Being a single dad made it that way, and the fact I loved her more than life itself meant I'd always do everything in my power to protect her.

Spotting the cherry red SUV my brother's girlfriend, Gracie, described on the phone, I watched as a blonde stepped out of the driver's side. Like a scene from a movie, I observed her walk toward me, the wind blowing through her long hair, my eyes glued to the sway of her curvy hips before moving up to watch her breasts bounce with each step. For a moment, I forgot the reason for her being there.

The squeeze of my daughter's hand on mine was a swift reminder. I needed to get my head in the game, make sure Gracie's best friend, Mary Jane, could truly look after Katelyn, and then haul ass to the hospital.

Quiet and shy, she squeaked out a timid, "Derrick?" with her eyebrows raised with hopefulness. Left speechless by her smile, I simply nodded. So much for getting my head in the game.

Turning to Katelyn, Mary Jane held out a plastic crown adorned with green, pink, and blue plastic jewels. "I found this and assumed it must be yours. You look like a princess who lost her tiara. Are you a princess?"

Katelyn grinned up at her. "It's not mine. I want to be a princess though."

Mary Jane looked around for a moment and shrugged. "Well, no one else here looks like a princess, so I think this belongs to you." Mary Jane helped Katelyn put the tiara on and fixed her hair to flow around it.

Their interaction was easy. I smiled when I looked at my girl and the blonde before me. Remembering myself, I cleared my throat and held out my hand. "Mary Jane, thanks so much for this."

She smiled at me and took my hand, giving a firm, short shake. "It's no problem."

When I'd received the call from Gracie about my brother's accident, she'd immediately suggested her best friend helping with Katelyn. She'd heard my hesitation through the pause but promised me her friend was safe and responsible. While I'd been gathering up my things and my daughter, wondering if we'd be heading straight to the hospital or to the park for her friend to babysit, she'd reassured me enough that I'd gratefully accepted.

Looking at the interaction playing out before me, I was damn pleased that I had.

"I mean it. If there're any issues, just call me."

"We'll be fine, won't we, Katelyn?" She reached out, and Katelyn immediately held her hand. I paused in surprise. Seeing my daughter take to this woman so easily was baffling. She'd always been shy around strangers, and it took a special person to bring out this side of her.

"Just let me know how Ash is when you have an update."

I nodded, having to shake myself to move. I needed to get to the hospital.

"Love you, Daddy," Katelyn said, giving me a small wave.

It seemed she was settled and eager for me to go. I smiled in relief, and Mary Jane covered her mouth to stifle her laughter.

"Give me a hug, and I'll get out of your hair."

Katelyn jumped up into my arms for a quick squeeze and then ran off to the swings. Keeping my eyes on my daughter, I said, "Thanks for doing this, Mary Jane."

She laughed again. "Honestly, it's fine. Go, and call me MJ. All my friends do. Tell Gracie I'm thinking about her and Ash and that I'll see her in a bit." She reached out and touched my hand lightly as she asked, "Are you calm enough to drive?" My eyes drifted down to her hand on mine. Sparks lit across my skin from her warm and comforting touch. Without thinking, I stroked her porcelain skin rhythmically, wondering how her soft skin would feel against my body. Coming out of my trance, I glanced up at her, and her cheeks flushed.

I cleared my throat. "I'm sorry. I don't know what I'm doing." I dropped her hand and then ran mine through my hair nervously. "I'll be fine to drive." I glanced at my watch. "I better get going. I'll call you and give you an update."

"Thanks." As I turned to leave, she called after me. "Um, Derrick?" Spinning back around, I moved a couple of steps closer to her. "It might help to have my number if you're going to call me."

Facepalm. Excellent move, Scarecrow, one day you'll get that brain. "Sorry, my mind's all over the place." An understatement if ever there was one. I set up a contact for her in my phone, then handed it to her to enter the number. Afterward, she pointed toward Katelyn, waved me goodbye, and headed over to the swings.

Just a few moments ago, I worried my drive to the hospital would be filled with angst over Ashton. Although I was concerned for him, my mind drifted back to Mary Jane. The subtle smell of her perfume wafted toward me in the wind. I'd been focused on her sincere smile when she arrived and even more so on her backside as she walked away from me.

My life revolved around my daughter. If I wasn't

working, I was with her. Most single guys my age were out drinking with friends or getting laid. As close as Ashton and I were, we didn't hang out too much in the evenings or without Katelyn being around. He and Gavin, our other brother, became part of Gracie's circle of friends when they met at a nightclub. Since they spent most nights at the club or drinking at the house shared with Gracie, Mary Jane, and Angel, I'd never had a chance to hang out with the group.

I'd met his girlfriend, Gracie, briefly one other time, when I stopped by his house one day. A hospital was not what I would've chosen for our first real conversation.

Once I arrived at the hospital, I was relieved to discover my brother was still in one piece, despite the cuts and bruises from his motorcycle accident, and I was able to release my built-up anxiety. I wrapped Gracie in a hug, and she broke down in my arms, whimpering Ashton's name. "Bad time for me to resemble him, I suppose." I attempted to lighten the mood with a joke.

To take our minds off the wait, we tried to make small talk. I used the opportunity to bring up the gorgeous blonde woman I couldn't get off my mind. "I was rather shocked when I saw MJ. That friend of yours is beautiful, and so sweet." Eyes widening, Gracie grinned like the Cheshire Cat.

Once Gracie caught wind of my interest in her friend, she encouraged me to pursue her. She'd promised to talk to Mary Jane about it herself after Ashton was better. While she went to check on him, I couldn't stop thinking about the blonde beauty. Since I had her number, I wasted no time in contacting her.

Me: Wanted to check on my girl. She's not too much trouble, is she?

Mary Jane: Not at all. She's a doll. How's Ashton?

Me: Sorry, I should've mentioned that first. He's fine. A bit banged up but nothing serious.

Mary Jane: Gracie holding up okay, then?

Me: She's great. I'll be there shortly to pick up Katelyn. Can I bring you anything to say thanks?

There was no response for a few minutes, making me wonder what I might have said. The bubbles on the phone showed she was texting. They stopped and started several times before one came through.

Mary Jane: Nothing needed.

Something made me wonder what she had typed out and decided not to send. After checking in personally with Ashton, who was in the midst of being discharged, I told Gracie I was headed out. Less than a mile down the road was a girl I needed to see again.

Katelyn's feet up in the air were all I could see with each push from Mary Jane on the swing. For a moment, I stood back to observe. Giggles from Katelyn filled the air to whatever words Mary Jane spoke to her.

"She seems quite content. I hate to interrupt the moment," I said as I stepped up next to Mary Jane.

Startled by my approach, she stumbled back a couple steps, and I grabbed her wrist to steady her. Long feminine fingers wrapped around the palm of my hand, securing the hold. "I didn't expect you back so soon."

Still holding her hand, I hoped she wouldn't pull away. It felt nice to be so close to someone; it had been too long.

"Daddy!" My dark-haired princess jumped off the swing and ran toward me. Lifting her up in my arms, I swung her around before peppering her face with kisses.

"Gracie is on her way with Uncle Ash. I told him you wanted to see him. Plus, his girlfriend, Gracie, wants to meet you. Stay here with MJ while I grab something from the car." Just as I grabbed my phone from the car, Gracie and Ashton pulled in. Noticing Gracie's smile, I turned to see what caught her attention. Mary Jane sat at the picnic table with Katelyn between her legs. Her fingers were twisting Katelyn's hair into a braid as my daughter rambled on about who knew what. It was said that the way to a man's heart was through his stomach, but the way to mine was through my daughter.

"I need to get Katelyn something to eat so we're going to head home. You need to go get some rest." Turning to Mary Jane, I said, "I'd love to treat you to a bite to eat as a thank you for earlier. If you're not busy?" Damn, why did this woman make me so nervous? In high school, I'd been such a smooth talker. It was how I ended up being a teenage dad.

"She grinned. "That'd be great. I'm free." With a rose tint to her cheeks, Mary Jane avoided eye contact while biting her lip. At least I wasn't the only one full of nerves.

For the past four years, Katelyn was the number one female in my life. No one came before her, no one ever would. Since Katelyn was born, I had gone on a date here or there, but nothing serious. No one even made it past a second date. At sixteen, when I heard I was going to be a father, it didn't come as completely bad news. Her mother wanted to put Katelyn up for adoption, but I couldn't let someone else raise my child.

Being a single dad wasn't a breeze by any means, but it wasn't something I'd trade for anything in the world. For the first time since she'd been alive, I saw the possibility of a relationship with a woman. The chemistry between this woman and my daughter was unmistakable.

I had no intention of wasting time and playing games. I wanted to get to know her. Katelyn had never met any of the few dates I had. It wouldn't have been fair to introduce people into her life if they weren't going to be permanent. It was too hard on a child. But it seemed Mary Jane was different. I intended to take things slow with her and to make sure Katelyn didn't get hurt in the process. I wasn't quite sure how I'd master that, but from one conversation, an immediate attraction, and the fact my girl had already met Mary Jane, it seemed natural that Katelyn would be involved, especially after the scare with her uncle.

We let Katelyn choose the place and wound up at Chuck E Cheese, a pizza place with a play area for children. The other entertainment consisted of large, rather disturbing, robotic animals that performed while we ate. When the music started up, Katelyn went to play with the other kids in the ball pit, leaving Mary Jane and me at the table alone.

"Is it just me or are those things creepy?" Mary Jane

asked with a sheepish look of embarrassment on her face.

"Totally creepy. How can a giant rat *not* be creepy?" When our waiter brought the pizza to our table, I motioned for her to go first. She picked up a steaming slice, strings of cheese trailing from the pan to the slice she chose, and brought it to her mouth. Her lips parted to blow lightly on the piece to cool it before wrapping around it and savoring the taste. She closed her eyes and gave a slight moan. Unconsciously, I licked my lips and shifted slightly in my chair. I tried to shrug it off; this was not the place to have lustful thoughts.

She opened her eyes and blushed when she noticed me staring. "Sorry. It's good."

"I can see that," I said with a smile. "Watching you eat it makes me want it even more." The pink filling her cheeks was adorable. She was shy and awkward, making her even more attractive. She exuded confidence without arrogance, which was sexy as hell. "So, you're in college with Gracie?" She nodded, so I continued. "What are you studying?"

"Engineering. I hope to get a job in the Imagineering program with Disney. That's my dream at least, to be able to learn some of the inner workings of a theme park so hugely creative and advanced. What about you? What do you do for a living?" When she wrapped her lips around the straw to take a drink of her soda, I wanted to be that straw.

Swallowing the thoughts in my head, I responded, "Security. Ashton does the club promoting, and I find security guards or bouncers. I'm a supervisor for a company that works most of the biggest clubs in town."

"Sounds pretty exciting."

"It can be. Mostly my job is paperwork and firing guys who aren't doing their job, so it can be a little boring. It's what I'm good at though. Ashton and I have talked about running our own club one day. I've been saving up for that in case it happens. Now that he's met Gracie, that may not be in the cards for us. Gracie seems like an amazing girl though. I'm happy for them."

"She is. We've been best friends since we were kids. If you could see her with Ashton, you'd know they're perfect together. It's unbelievably sweet and inspiring." She veered off that topic to one I wasn't expecting. "Can I ask what happened to Katelyn's mom?" Mary Jane cleared her throat and quickly said, "Forget I asked. That was rude."

"No, it's fine. We were kids, only sixteen when she found out she was pregnant. We were both scared at what it meant for our futures. She decided she didn't want a baby, and I decided I didn't want anyone else raising my child. Ashton thought I was nuts when I said I wanted full custody. He was the first one to tell me how wrong he was about that though. Katelyn's never met her mom." I paused, not sure if I should have held that back. It was rare I shared anything about my personal life, especially about Katelyn, but Mary Jane's wide eyes and reassuring smile kept me going. "The last time I saw her was the day at the hospital when she signed over custody to me... the day Katelyn was born. Even though she gave up her rights, I told her she could call anytime. I'd never intentionally keep her out of Katie's life. She's never even called to check on her or asked for pictures."

Mary Jane listened intently to each detail, glancing back over her shoulder occasionally to check on Katelyn. "It's her loss. She's missing out on a fantastic little girl," Mary Jane said, smiling at me. "It also shows a lot of character for you as a teenage boy to take on that responsibility."

The way she kept checking on Katelyn made it hard to fight my attraction, not that I wanted too, but the last thing Katelyn or I needed was to rush into something. Though, anyone who put my child first won points with me.

"I used to think I was an idiot for not being safe with my girlfriend and getting us both into that situation. On Katie's first birthday, I thought back to everything over that year and realized it wasn't a 'situation' I got us into. She is the best thing that ever happened to me." I paused a moment, second-guessing the seriousness of the conversation. "Sorry, didn't mean to get so personal."

"No, don't apologize. I love listening to you talk about your daughter. The way your face lights up shows what a great dad you are. It's very sexy." Her cheeks instantly warmed.

We were saved from the moment as Katelyn ran up to the table. "I'm hungry, Daddy!"

Lifting her up onto my lap, I hugged her and said, "Well, let's get some pizza in you before it gets cold." She turned to face forward and stayed on my lap as she lunged to grab a slice of pizza off the tray. Each time Katelyn took a bite, she offered the slice to me for the next bite. Together we finished three slices before Katelyn ran back out to play with other kids her age. "That girl can almost eat more than I can. Of course, she has three times my energy to burn it off too." Propping my elbow on the table, I rested my head on my hand. "Are you close to your parents?"

"My mom passed away when I was in high school, freshman year. Car accident. Dad remarried a few years later. He lives in Maine with my stepmother. I don't see them too much." Mindlessly stirring her drink, she appeared to distance herself from emotions when speaking of her family. "Occasional calls, e-mails mostly with jokes, the typical birthday card in the mail. That's about all there is. The great thing about my friendship with Gracie, Angel, and Cameron is they're my family." Peering up at me beneath long dark lashes, she smiled. "What about your parents?"

"I'm quite blessed with an amazing family. Obviously, you've met my older brother. Ashton is not only my brother but also my best friend. He was the first one I told about Katie. Calling me crazy and stupid was his first response of course, but he supported me from day one." Pausing a moment, I glanced around to make sure I could still spot Katelyn. She caught me looking and gave me a wave. "My parents spoil Katie beyond belief. We're the typical TV sitcom family. Kind of boring, isn't it?" I chuckled at how cliché my life sounded.

"Sounds wonderful. Reminds me of when I was younger and my mom was alive. Before she died, we had family dinners together. We celebrated every holiday with style. I miss my mom and having the nuclear family." This time her eyes glistened over with memories of her past. "Don't get me wrong, I love my new traditions with my friends too."

"It's not the same. I get it. Don't worry, it'll be our secret," I said with a wink. With her head lowered, I placed my hand on top of hers. Mary Jane looked up at me and smiled.

Before I could make a move, Katelyn came up and laid her head on my arm. "Daddy, I'm ready to go home." Kissing her forehead, I lifted her up into my arms.

"Someone needs a nap." Reaching into my pocket, I pulled out my wallet to leave enough cash to cover the bill and tip. "I'm sorry to end this so soon, but I need to get her home."

When I dropped Mary Jane off at her car, I stepped outside while Katelyn napped in the back seat.

"Thanks for dinner."

"It was my pleasure. Thank you for taking care of my girl."

"I enjoyed—"

"I would—"

After trying to speak at the same time, we both laughed. When she motioned for me to go ahead, I didn't argue. "I would like to see you again. On a more personal level." Her finger swiped a loose strand of hair and tucked it behind her ear. Biting her lip, she grinned.

"Sure, I'd love to."

"I'll call you and set something up?" With a nod, she gave me a wave before getting into her car and driving away. I wanted to press her against the door and taste those beautiful lips of hers. Instead, I waved goodbye.

Chapter Two

DERRICK

Over the next few nights, each time Mary Jane crossed my mind, I sent her a text. It was usually something random, trying to work my way up to the date. Each time I chickened out. Something about her made me a nervous wreck.

Me: Have you ever watched the movie Sharknado?

Mary Jane: No?

Me: Does that mean you're unsure?

Mary Jane: I'm unsure why you're asking

Me: It's like a trainwreck you can't look away from. We should watch it together sometime. This was my subtle way of leading into making plans with her.

Mary Jane: Will that be our date?

Me: No, I'm too classy for that. ;) Which reminds me, are you free tomorrow night?

Mary Jane: I'm free every night lately.

Me: I plan on changing that.

We made plans to meet at Ashton's house so I could drop Katelyn off there for them to babysit, and Mary Jane said she could have Gracie help with her hair. Girl bonding at its best. Pulling into the driveway, I smiled as I spotted her car. Inside, after a short conversation with Ashton, Gracie appeared by herself. "Is something wrong with MJ?"

Before she could answer, Mary Jane stepped into the room wearing a black dress, low cut in the front with a flowing skirt. "You look beautiful," I said, holding out a pink carnation. After saying goodbye to Katelyn, we walked out the door.

For our second date, the first official one I supposed, we went to a restaurant. Part of the time, we had so much to talk about, but I discovered she could also be quiet and reserved. When Mary Jane excused herself to the ladies' room, I called Ashton to check on Katelyn and ask Gracie for advice. She told me Mary Jane was a bit shy at first but to not give up. After asking a few questions, I came up with an idea that didn't require talking. I took care of the bill and planned the next part of our evening.

When she returned, I stood up before she could take a seat. "I paid the check. Are you up for what I have planned next or are you ready to go home?"

"I'm not tired. Show me what you've got."

She didn't know how dangerous those words could be at the moment, especially considering the dress she wore that exposed a few inches of silky smooth thigh begging to be caressed. Part of me wanted to disregard my manners and upbringing. It took all the restraint I had to keep from pressing her against the wall and showing her how sexy she was.

Lightly placing my hand on the small of her back, I led her out the door and then slipped my hand into hers. Leaving the restaurant in the heart of downtown, we took a walk along the central strip, joining the tourists and night owls looking for a decent dancing club. Stepping into a country-western bar off Second Avenue, Mary Jane paused to look around. "What are we doing here?"

"When I called to check on Katelyn earlier, I asked Gracie a few questions. She told me you like to country line dance. Was I misinformed?" I asked her with a smile and a wink.

"No, you weren't. I don't do it much anymore though."

Donning my sexiest grin, I attempted to persuade her with my charms. "Please, for me?"

Shoulders relaxed, she placed her palm out for me. We stepped out on the floor with the rest of the crowd, and I followed her lead as she showed me a few of the steps to go along with the song playing. Shuffling our feet to the music, tapping our heels, and sliding around, I picked up the dance rather quickly thanks to her excellent instruction.

After dancing for about an hour, we were both laughing at each other and ourselves. Watching her enjoy the music, the way her body moved to the beat, and the smile playing on her lips were all incredibly sexy. Beads of sweat trickled down her neck, falling into her cleavage, directing my eyes to follow the trail and notice how the dress stuck to every curve.

Unable to hold back, I grabbed her hand and dragged her over to the corner where I pushed her against the wall. Pressing my mouth against hers softly at first, the passion between us quickly ignited. Her hands tangled in my hair as she pulled me closer. Hitching her leg around my waist, my body instantly responded to hers. Unable to disguise the effect she had on me, I grabbed her hips and ground against her to let her feel my want. It had been too long since I'd been with a woman. Uncontrollable desire tore through me as her tongue circled mine. Mary Jane moaned into my mouth, and I groaned in return. "Let's go to the car."

Carelessly sprinting down the sidewalk and dashing across the street, we raced to the parking lot two blocks away. When I opened the back door, she slid in first and waited for me. I slipped in, locked the doors behind me, and moved my mouth to her neck. Her skin tasted like the sweet nectar of a honeysuckle; I wanted more of her. Grasping her around the waist, I pulled her tighter against me. After scratching her nails down my back slowly, she lifted my shirt and ran her fingernails over my bare skin.

"Mary Jane," I moaned as my lips found the swell of her breast. Cursing the dress for covering her so snuggly, I slid my hand up her leg, pushing higher until I felt her lace panties. Leaning back to look at her, I whispered, "Damn, MJ, you're beautiful."

She pulled me back to her mouth. "Touch me," she begged. Obeying her, my fingers slipped inside her panties, and she threw her head back and gasped as they found her sensitive nub. With my chest heaving with desire, I watched her pleasure as my hands brought her to climax. Her legs clamped down on my hand as she came in a fierce orgasm that shook her entire body. Suddenly her cheeks burned crimson, and her eyes bulged in horror. "I'm sorry," she said as she sat up and fixed her dress.

"For what?" I asked. "That was the sexiest thing I've ever witnessed."

"Really?" she asked, honestly surprised, the smile reappearing where it had faded momentarily.

"Yes, MJ. You're incredibly sexy, but I'm sorry if I went too far tonight."

Mary Jane palmed my face. "You didn't. I mean, I've never done this before, but it was amazing."

"Never done what before?"

At that moment, she crawled back into her shy, awkward state again. "I'm… um… I think I want to go home." She stepped out of the back seat of the car and moved to the front passenger's seat.

Mary Jane's silence on the drive home filled me with worry that I'd screwed up a good thing before it had a chance to get started. When we reached Ashton and Gracie's, I walked her to the door and stopped a few feet before it. "I'm sorry if I offended you. I never meant to."

"No. You didn't. Tonight was amazing, every part of it." She took a deep breath, closed her eyes, and admitted what she couldn't admit to me before. "I'm a virgin. In fact, I haven't done much more than simple kissing before. If you think I'm a freak, I'll understand."

I pulled her in for a kiss; my lips lightly brushed hers

at first. As I gently slid my tongue along her bottom lip, she invited me into her mouth by parting her lips to allow access. She released a pleasure-filled sigh, and it made me want a repeat of earlier. Now that I knew the truth though, I needed to take things slower.

"You're not a freak. I'm honored to have given you your first orgasm," I said softly against her lips. She quivered as I said this, so I added, "I'll make all your firsts special if you let me."

"If you keep talking like that, I'm going to have another orgasm right here," she said nervously. It turned me on more to hear this shy woman say something dirty to me. "And the *first* I experienced tonight was very special."

After that night, things seemed to be going great as far as Mary Jane and I were concerned. Ashton had been doing better since his crash, though they were still dealing with Gracie's stalker ex-boyfriend. They kept a lot of the details from us, but Ashton had told me enough to understand it was a bad situation.

When Ashton asked me to train Gracie to shoot a gun, I used the opportunity for another date with Mary Jane. I enjoyed each minute. I also wanted to help Gracie out. After doing security for the last couple of years, I had gotten my armed license because it helped me get better paying jobs. For my twenty-first birthday, a few months ago, I obtained a concealed carry permit. Armed security paid two to three times the salary. Raising a girl on my own, I needed to make sure I had a steady income and could build a decent savings account for her future.

The day at the range, when Gracie's ex showed up with a gun and I ended up shot, changed all our lives. Mary Jane's face when I hit the ground stuck in my mind. I'd never seen such fear in her eyes, such despair on her face. After we had survived that, we had our fourth or fifth dates. And after that, I'd stopped counting.

I'd planned to keep Katelyn separate from our dating, thinking it would make Mary Jane more comfortable. Instead, she began making plans to include Katelyn. They'd grown close. Mary Jane even gave her the nickname of Katie-cat. The bond between the two of them had become so strong it made everything seem almost too good to be true. And then things took a turn I didn't expect.

CHAPTER THREE

MARY JANE

Most people fall in love several times over a lifetime, but one always sticks out more than others, whether you end up with them or they are the one who got away.

When I was five, I thought I was in love with my best friend, Jimmy, who lived next door. That changed when he fed my favorite Barbie doll to the dog, breaking my heart. When I was ten, I fell for my schoolmate Robbie when he helped me up after someone pushed me into the mud. My heart later shattered when my dad told me we were moving to the big city of Nashville from our small backwoods town in Kentucky, and I had to say goodbye to him. At fifteen, I fell for Marcus Jacobs, the smartest guy in school. He was our valedictorian, and I never told him how I felt. He "came out of the closet" after high school. And then I turned twenty-one and met Derrick Collins.

Derrick was the guy who made me realize that I'd never known love before I met him. Reading about toes-tingling, heart-stopping kisses, and romantic gestures, I always questioned whether such things existed. My lifelong question was answered the first time we kissed, and I felt it course through my body from my lips straight to my toes with electric pulses racing everywhere in between.

Growing up, I always had an issue with weight and never felt comfortable with the opposite sex. Puberty hit and my waistline expanded more than my breasts. Luckily, I had a growth spurt around sixteen. I was taller than average, five eight to be exact, with blonde hair and light green eyes, with that I was happy. My pants size was a different story. My hips were curvy, and my breasts caught up to them, although they didn't point forward as much as my hips pointed outward.

With friends like mine who built my confidence every day, I thought I knew what it meant to feel beautiful. It wasn't until the day I felt Derrick's undeniable passion for me that I truly felt like the goddess Cameron always tried to convince me I was. I'd tried every diet known to man to be skinny; it just was not in the cards for me, and I'd come to terms with that fact. My body may not have been perfect, but I ate right, and I wasn't lazy. It was just my luck I had a crappy metabolism that allowed me to maintain a softer, slightly rounder stomach. Did it frustrate me? Yes. I would've loved to be one of those women who ate anything they wanted and never gained a pound. However, life didn't deal me that hand, and I'd become content with myself.

It's true that having a boyfriend wasn't the most important thing in life, but it sure was nice. I loved my time with Derrick. I didn't need him to make me happy; I wanted it. Derrick made the sky bluer, chocolate taste sweeter, and the sun shine brighter, at least it seemed that way with him in my life. Prince Charming had nothing on this man. At times I became discouraged, but Derrick was there to make me laugh. Other than Cameron, no other man had told me I was beautiful in a way that made me believe it. He was practically perfect in every way, like a male version of Mary Poppins. Wow, that wasn't sexy I guess, but if Derrick was one thing for sure, it was sexy.

The day I received my acceptance letter for the internship at Disney should have been the best day of my life. I was incredibly proud of achieving that amazing accomplishment. However, on the other hand, I knew it meant I had to leave Derrick and Katelyn behind.

As soon as the shock wore off, I called Derrick. "We need to talk."

"That doesn't sound good. Is everything all right, sweetheart?" Closing my eyes, I wanted to cry, but I held back. Holding onto hope was all I could do. "It's fine. There's something I received in the mail today I want to show you."

"Come on over. Katelyn's at her grandparents, so we have the place to ourselves for a while." I knew it would be easier to discuss without Katelyn interrupting, for that I was thankful.

Derrick must have heard me pull up because he opened the door before I could knock. Pulling me forward, his lips met mine, and I could taste the flavor of his favorite mint. Without breaking the kiss, we stumbled our way across the room to his couch. Plopping down on the couch, I landed softly on him, feeling his passion ignite. With my hands pressed against his chest, I pushed myself up. "As much as I love this, we need to talk."

Derrick sat up with me, the smile on his face still brightening the room. "Talk to me, beautiful. You said you got something in the mail?"

"Read this, it will explain everything." Taking the letter, I watched as he skimmed it. As he read it, I noticed how his face lit up after the first few lines.

"Congratulations, MJ. This is amazing!" Pointing to the letter again, I waited as he kept reading. His face fell, and he glanced up at me. "You leave so soon? For two years?" With a nod, I glanced down to avoid seeing his face. "Not a big deal, we'll make it work."

"Make what work, Derrick?"

"Us. This." He gestured between us with his hands. "Long-distance relationships can work."

"You have Katelyn. It would never work."

"I haven't been in a relationship since Katelyn came into my life. If anything, this will give me more time with her again." His reasoning made sense in a way, but I still wasn't convinced.

"For me, it's best for us to just end this now before it gets too serious." The words tasted like ash in my mouth.

My feelings for Derrick were stronger than I'd ever felt for anyone else. I had gone beyond too serious. Not wanting to give him much room to argue, I stood and walked to the door. "I'm sorry, Derrick. These last few weeks have been wonderful. I love Katelyn and… I'll miss you both so much."

"Mary Jane—"

I walked out before letting him finish. From there I went to dinner with Gracie, Angel, and Cameron to give them the news.

In the next few weeks, I said my goodbyes and packed up my life.

When I told Derrick about the internship at Disney, he fought for us to stay together, and that meant the world to me. Nonstop calls, showing up at our friends' house to talk to me, he even showed up the day I left to give me a gift. It was a baby blue hand-painted coffee mug with a pink handprint and the words "I love you" written in black. Inside the cup were movie stubs, a pink carnation, and a couple of Chuck E Cheese tokens. "I added those to remind you of me. I won't forget our time together, and I hope you don't either," Derrick said to me just before I planted a long, passionate goodbye kiss to those sweet lips of his.

So, Angel and I loaded up our cars and moved our life to Orlando, Florida leaving behind our friends who'd become family and quite possibly the love of my life.

Chapter Four

DERRICK

Shortly after Mary Jane left for Florida, I hopped on a flight to New York for Ashton and Gracie's wedding. They had a double wedding with Cameron and Gavin. The legalization of gay marriage was still new, and in states like Tennessee, it was difficult to find someone to officiate over same-sex marriages due to being in, what was referred to as, the Bible belt. Cameron wanted to avoid any conflict, so they chose New York as a wedding locale.

As happy as I was for my brother, watching the two of them profess their love for one another wasn't on my list of fun things to do. My mind was filled with what could have been with Mary Jane. I'd made it four years without a girlfriend; it should be a breeze to go two more. My biggest fear was she'd fall in love with someone else while away.

She wanted to be at the wedding. I'd asked her to be my date before she received her letter, but she had to cancel when the date of her internship fell two days before the wedding would take place. It broke Mary Jane's heart to miss one of her closest friend's big day.

My parents took care of Katelyn while Ashton and I spent his last few single hours together. "So, you're ready to give up the bachelor life?" I asked, nudging him with my elbow.

"With everything Gracie and I have been through, I can't believe we made it this far." The dreamy look in his eyes made my mind wander off to Mary Jane. I imagined her wearing a white gown, surrounded by roses, walking toward me down a long aisle.

"I need alcohol. Can I raid the mini bar?"

"Cameron's paying, so—"

"So, yes, then. Great!" I pulled a small bottle of vodka from the mini bar and downed it in one swallow.

"Damn. Something you want to talk about, little brother?" Ashton asked, closing the mini fridge just as I pulled out the second tiny bottle of vodka.

"Gracie's fantastic, Ash, and I'm incredibly happy for you. After Addy's death and everything you went through to recover from that, you deserve to be happy." Addy was Ashton's first love, killed during a robbery at a convenience store.

"But?" Ashton asked, grabbing a bottle of Jack Daniel's out of the fridge.

"No buts. It gives me a little hope that one day I'll get

that happiness. I just hoped it would be with MJ."

"Who says it can't?"

"Life. Fate. It all stands against me."

"You're being dramatic, Derrick. She's a ten-hour drive away. I've gotten to know MJ since meeting Gracie. She told you it wouldn't work because she's scared. For one, she doesn't want to take you away from Katelyn. And I've heard her speak about you. She looks at you the way Gracie looks at me. Don't wait as long as I did to notice. Fight for the girl you love." Ashton made everything clear to me. After the wedding, I would do everything I could to convince Mary Jane we deserved a chance.

Like something out of a magazine, the wedding was perfect. My brother had never looked so happy. Much of the wedding I viewed through my phone as I captured every angle of Katelyn in her flower-girl dress. Being the proud dad, I couldn't miss a moment.

During the flight back to Nashville, Katelyn sat with her grandparents, so I had a little time to think. I considered the pros and cons of a long-distance relationship. In the end, the pros outweighed the cons by a landslide, so I went over everything I wanted to say to Mary Jane.

At home, I put Katelyn to bed and texted Mary Jane immediately.

Me: Do you have a minute to talk?

Mary Jane: Sure.

"Hey. How was the move?" I asked as soon as she

answered the phone.

"It wasn't bad. We have a cute little apartment here. I miss everyone so much. I'm thankful to have Angel though." Being perky was the norm for Mary Jane, not the sad tone I caught in her voice during this call. "How was the wedding?" she asked.

"Beautiful. Gracie looked gorgeous, as did Katelyn of course. I've never seen Ashton as happy as he is with Gracie. I'm glad he met her, and selfishly I'm glad that I met you because of their union." She didn't respond, and I was worried I scared her off. "You got quiet, did I say something wrong?"

"No, of course not. It's just… I miss you so much." She said those last five words so fast I thought I misunderstood her. Then she repeated herself. "I miss you, Derrick, more than anything else."

"Why are we not trying the long-distance thing again?" I asked, genuinely confused and hoping desperately that she felt the same uncertainty.

"It would be too confusing for everyone, especially Katelyn. If it didn't work out—"

I stopped her before she could finish the thought. "Why wouldn't it work out? I think we have a great shot at having what Ash and Gracie have. What if we keep it our little secret? We could see what happens and leave everyone else out. We can date on our own terms without other people interfering or giving friendly advice, the typical things that can kill a relationship by causing unwanted thoughts of insecurity."

"I'm not sure how often I can visit between my internship and studying to finish my degree. You can't exactly drop everything to come see me either." She was right; it would be a challenge. But I'd face any challenge thrown at me to get more time with this sweet, southern woman to whose charm I'd succumbed.

"It doesn't matter, sweetheart. We can Skype, do Facetime, talk on the phone, whatever it takes. I'll wait for you because you're worth it." I meant that 100 percent. Obviously, intimacy is important in a relationship and easier when you reside in the same state. None of that mattered though. I knew what I wanted, and it was Mary Jane. We could take things slow to be sure she was ready for whatever came next.

The elation in her voice rose. "You think we can do this?"

"Yes, I do. And we could still be intimate in different ways. Sexy Skype, Freaky Facetime, phone sex…."

She gave a sexy laugh. "You make me believe that we can make this work."

"What would you say to scheduling a Skype date for your next day off?"

"Sounds perfect." For the next half hour, we exchanged work schedules and made plans for our first two dates.

Hanging up the phone, I felt better than I had in weeks. I tossed my phone onto the couch, stood up, and gave a shout of excitement. My hands flew up to cover my mouth; I had forgotten Katelyn was asleep. I walked over to the bottom of the stairs and listened for movement. Luckily, I hadn't woken her.

After that day, we took every opportunity to talk. We led our friends to believe we decided to keep our relationship on the *friends level* for the time being. One of us always sent a text to check the coast was clear if we wanted to talk on the phone. We had a couple of close calls for people finding us out. Sneaking around offered more excitement in a way.

One afternoon, a month later, I stayed home sick from work. Lying in bed trying to get over this funky feeling, I flipped through channels looking for something to keep me occupied. As usual, among three hundred channels of cable, there was nothing watchable on.

Glancing at my watch, I noticed it was only nine in the morning. It would be ten in Orlando, and Mary Jane's schedule had her working afternoons that week. Since Katelyn was at pre-school for a few hours, it would be the perfect time for us to spend a couple of good long hours together. Without another thought, I dialed Mary Jane's number.

"Hey, sweetheart, do you work today?"

"Nope, took the day off to study and relax a bit. You sound terrible, what's wrong?"

"You know how to sweet talk a guy. I'm not feeling great, so I stayed home from work. I think it's a sinus infection or something equally as sexy. If you aren't busy, I'd like to take you on a date. A perk of the long-distance situation is I won't give you any germs I may have."

She was quiet. I could imagine her eyebrows scrunched

in confusion and her chewing on the side of her lip in thought. "How exactly are we going to do that?"

I laughed and said, "Let's Skype and eat together. Then I thought we could sit and watch a movie. What do you think?"

She sighed. "I think that sounds perfect."

We managed to have many of the same ingredients in our pantry, so we created the same meal, and I sat the laptop across the table from me while we talked via Skype. It was almost like sitting at the table with her. "You look beautiful."

She stroked her fingers through her hair, checking it over. "I've barely been out of bed. I'm still in my pajamas. Angel said I'd been cooped up too much since we got here, so we went to a club and were out until three in the morning." All I could see was the top half of her, covered by a spaghetti strap tank top. Being a typical guy, I mostly noticed her cleavage ready to spill out at any moment. It wasn't a bad thing to appreciate an unbelievably sexy woman.

"Pajama pants?" I asked, wanting to get a full picture in my mind, hoping for my table's sake she wasn't only wearing panties. If that were the case, I worried I might knock a notch in the bottom of this table at any moment.

As soon as she stood, I hardened, and table knocking wasn't far off. She had on shorts fitted to her form. Unaware of her sex appeal, she nonchalantly waved her arms and said, "Shorts, the heat down here, even in October, is too much to sleep in pants. Even with the air conditioning on, I wake up in the morning with everything sticking to me. It's not the most attractive outfit, but you caught me off guard."

She wrapped her arms around herself in an attempt to cover her state of undress. "Maybe I should put on a robe. I'm sure the camera makes me look bigger than you even remember."

The moment she talked about waking up with her clothes sticking to her from the heat, all I could think about was undressing her and working up a sweat in the best possible way. Shaking my head to clear my thoughts, I said, "What? No. You look beautiful. I… well… let's just say I *really* wish I were there right now. I didn't expect to see you in such a sexy outfit."

She blushed. "Sexy? This?" Extending her arms, she spun in a circle to give me a breathtaking view of her entire body in motion. I adjusted in my seat, cleared my throat, and looked away.

"You're killing me, babe." With a sexy smile, she blew me a kiss, and I licked my lips as the need to taste her overcame me. I'd have given anything to have her here so I could remove those sexy pajamas myself. "Excuse me a minute." Stepping into my kitchen, I ran the faucet until it was as cold as I could handle, and then I stuck my head underneath it.

She giggled softly as she saw my wet hair when I returned. "Are you better now?"

"Are you here with me?" That was meant to let her know how much I wanted her; instead, it brought us both to reality. "I'm sorry, that was stupid to say."

"No, it was sweet. I wish I could be there." An Awkward silence followed while we both tried to eat our breakfast. After a few minutes, I asked, "What movie would you like to watch?"

"Well, something we both have would be Disney movies; how about the newest release?" My thoughts made me chuckle. "That would be the safest type of movie we could watch for me personally."

She covered her mouth, softening a laugh. "Sounds good to me too."

We curled up in our separate beds; hers looked more inviting than mine. "You look pretty comfy over there in your bed surrounded by pillows," I said as I pulled up the scratchy afghan my grandmother made me years ago.

"I'd be comfier if you were here curled up with me." Both of us had strategically placed our laptops so we could watch the movie but still see each other.

For the next hour and a half, I watched Mary Jane as she watched the movie. I took in everything about her. Her soft pink lips were puckered in thought during the serious scenes. During the funny scenes, she would throw her head back in laughter. "Are you even watching the movie?" she asked, suddenly bringing me out of my stupor to notice she was staring back at me now.

"What? Um, yeah, of course. She's found Prince Charming now, right?" I was oblivious to the plot of this movie. I'd bought it for Katelyn but had yet to watch it with her. I loved Disney movies, but right then I couldn't take my eyes off this woman or stop wishing that I were in bed with her.

That perfect giggle of hers sounded again. "There's no Prince Charming in this one."

Pulling the comforter back, she sat up, putting her chest in full view of the camera. "MJ, honey, move back a bit."

She gasped. "Oh, sorry!"

"Nothing to be sorry for, it just makes me think of that old slogan 'reach out and touch someone,' but I can't." If I could, we'd have been rolling around in that bed right then without the hindrance of clothes. The long-distance stuff was harder than I thought.

Mary Jane looked away and called out, "Hey, girl, be right there." Turning back to the camera, she whispered, "I gotta go. Angel's home. I had a great date."

"Me too. We'll talk later." She blew me a kiss, and I pretended to catch it and press it to my lips. Cheesy, I know, but it was still romantic, and I'd give this woman as many cheesy moments as she wanted.

The screen went blank on her end, and I was left staring at a black display in sadness for a moment. Though I was happy to be able to talk to Mary Jane, being unable to touch her was harder than I expected. Just the thought of holding her in my arms while we watched a movie made the loneliness worse. Every day I worried she might meet a guy down there who would give her what I couldn't right then. My daughter had always meant the world to me; she was the only person who kept me from driving to Florida.

Slowly, I closed my laptop lid and slid further into the bed until my body lay flat. Rolling over, I grabbed a pillow and hugged it to my body as I drifted off to sleep with dreams of Mary Jane dancing through my head—rather dirty dreams.

CHAPTER FIVE

MARY JANE

Lunchtime rolled around, and as usual, I went into the lounge to sit by myself and read. Meeting new people was never an easy task for me. If they didn't approach me first, I usually didn't speak for fear of rejection, I suppose.

I was enjoying—using the word enjoying lightly—my lean microwave meal that was a portion big enough for a squirrel to fill up on, when I felt the table shift and glanced up. A giant blue monster with purple spots sat across from me, he lifted a furry arm to wave. I snickered and waved back. "I love your movies. Where's your little green one-eyed friend?"

His large form shook with laughter as he removed the head of the costume so he could speak. I almost choked on my food at the sight of the handsome man behind the mask.

Extending a large, furry, blue hand, he introduced himself. "I'm Tristan. I'm not really a monster; I only play one. I'd like to say on TV, but alas, my acting career hasn't taken off as I hoped it would. Perhaps the blue fur causes me to be typecast?"

He winked at me, and I shook his hand. "Nice to meet you. I'm Mary Jane. Most people call me MJ." Tristan had lightly bronzed skin, and his shaved head looked a bit odd on him, but I didn't judge. His eyes were green with light specks of brown in the mix.

Releasing a heavy breath, he sighed. "Whew, wearing this thing is tougher than it looks."

Feeling the sticky heat dampening my skin as I wore a button-down shirt and shorts, I empathized with his plight. "Can't you change out of it?"

He nodded. "Once my shift is through. I'm covering for the guy who's supposed to be taking my place. Let's keep that our little secret though, if you don't mind. I don't want to get him in trouble."

I held up my index finger and then made an X over my heart. "Cross my heart and hope to die."

He shivered. "That is one of the creepiest sayings, especially when you follow it up with the *stick a needle in my eye* portion. What were people thinking when they said these things?" I laughed before taking another bite of my lunch.

He leaned forward, glancing at my plate and then up at me. "Is that a snack?"

I shook my head. "Nope, it's lunch."

His eyes bulged. "Sweetheart, that isn't lunch for anyone. What time do you get off today?"

I thought about that for a moment. "Around six?"

He nodded. "Great, me too. Let's grab dinner somewhere. I need more friends around here, and from the looks of it, you do too. Am I right?"

I sighed. "Is it that obvious?" In the three months I'd been there, I'd yet to make a single friend. My coworkers were nice enough, but it was mostly a "Good Morning" and "How are you?" kind of conversation we had each day.

He shrugged. "Well, you did get excited to see a big blue monster sit down with you." Standing up, he placed the giant head back over his face. Through the mask, he mumbled, "I'll meet you at the front gates around six."

Well, that seemed promising. It'd be the first time I had dinner with someone other than Angel since I moved to Florida. Tonight was a perfect night too since Angel was doing out-of-town training for her job this week. Tristan seemed cool, and he wasn't bad to look at either. My phone dinged with a text, bringing an even bigger grin to my face.

Derrick: Hope you're having a great day. I was sitting here thinking about you.

Me: I miss you. Going to have dinner with a friend tonight. Can we talk after?

Derrick: Definitely. No matter what time, I want to hear your beautiful voice. Where are you going for dinner?

As soon as his text came in, I was called away to help a coworker and swore to myself I'd text him back when I was done. Six o'clock rolled around, and I made my way to the front of the park to wait for Tristan. Six fifteen rolled around, no Tristan. Strolling into a nearby gift shop, I picked up a few small trinkets for Katelyn. Since I'd been here, I'd kept in touch with her by sending a package with a note in it every week. Derrick said she would bounce to the mailbox every day, and when he heard her squeal, he knew one of my packages had arrived.

When six thirty came, and he still hadn't arrived, I decided to go on home. As I pushed through the exit, I heard someone calling out. "MJ!" Tristan was running down the main street of the park toward me, waving his arm in the air. Once he caught up, he bent to place his hands on his knees while he caught his breath. "Damn, girl, I don't usually run unless I'm being chased by a serial killer, so you should feel honored, because seriously, that never happens."

I rested my hand over my heart. "I feel very honored, sir." Moving my hand to my hip, I said, "I didn't think you were going to show. Why so late?"

"My apologies. Getting out of my suit was a nightmare, and my relief was late. I'll make it up to you with a fantastic meal tonight." Instead of going to the parking lot, he grabbed my hand and tugged me toward the monorail system.

"I'm scared of heights. I'm not sure I want to ride that!"

Tristan squeezed my hand. "You can hold my hand the entire time if you need to. It's a cool ride, I promise."

If I wanted to be friends with this man, I had to put some trust into him. "Okay, where are we going?"

He smiled. "It's a surprise, but I promise you one thing,

you're about to get laid." With those simple words, I panicked a bit, thinking this was a date instead of a friendly dinner like I thought. I worried I'd misjudged or possibly misunderstood Tristan's intentions, but I didn't want to make an idiot of myself and ask what he meant. Anxiety wracked my body as we got off at one of the resorts.

Rounding the corner, understanding slapped me in the face. A girl in a Hawaiian skirt and bikini top came up and placed a lei over my head, he snickered. "You should've seen your face earlier… priceless."

Smacking him playfully, I realized his sense of humor was a lot like Cameron's. "So, what are we doing?"

He grinned. "We're watching the luau and having dinner. The guy I covered for paid me by giving me tickets for tonight. I was going to sell them because I wasn't going to come by myself, and then I met you, so it worked out nicely."

As he pulled out a seat for me, Tristan said, "Tell me about the guy." With my eyebrow cocked and mouth agape, I waited for clarification on the guy he wanted information on. "The guy who you're so into. The look on your face earlier was a mixture of panic and guilt. So, spill."

"Derrick! Oh my gosh, I forgot to text him back!" I pulled my phone out and sent a quick message.

Me: Sorry I didn't answer sooner; I was working. I'm at a luau dinner at one of the resorts. I'll call you tonight. Miss you. Give Katie-cat a hug for me.

Tristan was reading over my shoulder and smirked. "Very sweet. Who is Katie-cat?"

"His daughter."

Tristan's eyebrow rose with curiosity, and he asked, "*His* daughter? Not your daughter together?"

I shook my head. "No, I wish she was my daughter. She's an awesome kid. He was only sixteen when he became a dad, and he's raised her on his own, with the occasional help of his parents and two brothers."

Tristan nodded in approval. "He sounds like a keeper."

I responded, "He is, otherwise I wouldn't even try this whole long-distance thing."

His eyebrows rose again. "Where does he live?"

"In Nashville, which is the city I moved here from."

Tristan nodded again, and then we were interrupted by our waitress. She grinned at Tristan. "Welcome, U'i. How are you?"

He blushed in response to her obvious flirting. "Great, you look well."

"You look pretty good yourself. On a date?" she asked, glancing over at me curiously. Tristan's cheeks reddened more before he said, "This is my new friend, MJ." Offering me a polite grin and nod, she dropped the conversation and took our drink orders, then moved to the next table.

"Friend of yours?" I asked. "And what did she call you?"

He pursed his lips as he seemed to choose his words carefully. "She's an ex-girlfriend, I guess. We ended on good terms though, so I like to think of her as a friend. She called me *U'i*. It's Hawaiian for handsome."

Glancing back at the waitress, I took in her appearance. She was of Hawaiian descent, or I assumed so from her beautiful coloring and features, and she was wearing a Hawaiian shirt with a straight khaki skirt. "She's cute, definitely more your type than I would be."

Tristan's face screwed up in confusion at the comment even I thought was odd of me to say. "Why is that exactly?" I shrugged because I had no answer for it. "So, you don't think sweet, country, rockin' hot blondes are my thing?"

Peering around the room, I tried to find the woman he was describing. "Who are you talking about?"

He laughed. "You need a mirror, darling girl. *You* are hot."

I rolled my eyes. "I hope you have a good vision plan, because you need glasses, sir." Lately, especially in this insufferable heat, I hadn't felt remotely attractive.

He turned to grab a guy walking by, who resembled the actor Ryan Gosling, and asked, "Would you date my friend here?"

Much to my humiliation, "Ryan" took a lingering glance over my body, stopped a moment to view the girls for a second time, and replied, "Hell yeah."

Tristan turned back to me. "See."

The guy leaned forward. "So, do I get your number?" Wiggling his eyebrows suggestively, he licked his lips and rubbed his palms together.

Tristan waved his hands in dismissal. "No, dude, you think a chick this hot is single? It was a rhetorical question, move on!" "Ryan" moved on looking a bit annoyed at being troubled for an answer since he wasn't getting anything in return. As I laughed at Tristan's dismissal of him, despite my heated cheeks, I couldn't help being flattered by the attention.

Over the next few hours, we filled up on Hawaiian sweet bread, grilled pineapple, ham, rice, and a dessert of molten lava cake. During the meal, a play was performed with several of the waitstaff participating along with volunteers chosen from the crowd. It was an enjoyable night; the only thing that would have made it better would've been Derrick's presence. Tristan was wonderful company, but the romantic ambiance of the show made me want my boyfriend beside me.

After the luau, neither of us were tired, so we set out to find a good spot to hang out. A lake with a beachfront feel to it, complete with sandy edges, sat next to the resort. We took over a couple of lounge chairs and sipped on the frozen margaritas that Tristan talked his lady friend into letting us take with us, with the promise we'd return the glasses. He was a sweet talker, no doubt about it.

Throughout the night, I noticed how he would run his hands back and forth across his bald head, so I finally asked, "Is that a new style for you?"

He glanced at his hand, as if suddenly realizing what he was doing, and laughed. "Yeah, it is. I usually keep it much longer; this is strange for me."

I nodded in understanding. "So why the bold choice to shave it?"

Tristan pulled out his cell phone. Then after a moment, he handed it to me. On the screen was a young girl whose hair was starting to grow in. She had a small bow resting on top of her head that had to have been fastened there with tape. "My little sister, Macy."

I went for the most logical assumption. "She's beautiful. Is it leukemia?"

His brow furrowed and he shook his head. "No, she doesn't have cancer. She's twelve and extremely intelligent—smart enough she's a sophomore in high school now. I've raised her on my own for the last three years. Our mom has early onset Alzheimer's, and our dad left years ago after she started to deteriorate. Mom's in a home now and doesn't remember who we are most of the time."

Thus far, his story didn't remotely answer the reasoning for the drastic hairdo, but I waited patiently for further details. After a moment, he continued by saying, "Due to her age, she's bullied pretty regularly by the older kids. One day at school, some girls cornered her in the bathroom and took a razor to her hair. They shaved it off in places, enough randomness there was nothing else to do but shave it completely. She called me in a panic, and I went to pick her up from school, not knowing what I was going to see when I arrived. She cried all night about how ugly she was and how she'd never show her face in public again. I calmed her down and made her take a nap. While she was sleeping, I shaved my head. She knew how much I loved my hair— yes, I admit I'm like a girl in that aspect. When she woke up and saw my head, she cried and told me I was the best brother in the world."

As his eyes welled with tears, I reached out and closed my hand over his. "I'm keeping it shaved until hers grows back fully because mine will take no time to grow. Her hair grows slower than mine. Sometimes she wears wigs, but it's still obvious." Our eyes met, and his frown deepened as he swiped his thumb under my eye to wipe away the tears. "Sorry, I didn't mean to bring you down."

Letting go of his hand, I lifted my shirt to dab my face dry. "It reminds me of my school days when I experienced similar treatment. My friends and I were all familiar with bullies. I received bullying in the form of verbal abuse for my weight. My roommate, Angel, was pushed around for being Hispanic. Gracie took the bullying brunt for being friends with us, and Cameron had the worst bullying because he's gay. I despise bullies." Many days I'd go home and consider ending my life due to bullies. If it hadn't been for Cameron, Gracie, and Angel, I might not have survived high school. Kids could be so cruel, especially with the abundance of social media making humiliation even worse.

Tristan stood up and moved his chair right next to mine, then wrapped his arms around me. We cuddled on the beach for a few minutes after he said, "Me too."

"You mentioned a roommate?" Tristan asked.

"Angel. When I received my letter for the internship, she offered to move with me."

"Wow. That's quite a sacrifice. What convinced her to give up everything and move with you? From the sounds of it, you have a pretty close group of friends back home." Thinking about my friends made me homesick, even with Angel so close. And December was the worst because it would be my first Christmas away from everyone.

"Her family is from Florida. We shared a three-bedroom house back home with our friend Gracie. Just before I found out about moving, Gracie got engaged and was going to move out. Angel wouldn't have had anywhere to live, and apartments are expensive in Nashville. She saved me a fortune by sharing rent with me too. And I'm shy, so it's nice to have a friend in town."

"Now you have two," he said, giving my shoulder a squeeze. I smiled and laid my head against him. Being comfortable around anyone so quickly wasn't in my nature. Something about Tristan, perhaps the way he reminded me of Derrick, helped ease the homesickness a little.

Realizing the lateness of the hour, we had to call it a night. Tristan ran our glasses back to his friend before we caught the last monorail back to the park. Tristan offered to drive me to my car for safety, and I gladly took him up on it. After pointing my car out to him, he stopped just behind it. "Well, we officially bonded tonight, I'd say." Doing his best valley girl impression, he said, "You know we'll have to be besties."

I chuckled. "I'd say that's an accurate description of the night. And I'd love to be your bestie. I'd like to meet your sister sometime. Maybe when I have a day off, she and I could hang out at the park?" Since I'd left Nashville, I'd missed Katelyn so much, I wanted to fill the void she left in my life. Macy seemed to need a friend as much as I did, and I wanted to be that for her.

Elated at the idea, his face brightened like a kid on Christmas morning. "She'd love that, MJ. Thank you. I'll set it up. Maybe we can both have the day off."

"Sounds great. Thanks for tonight. I needed it more than you know." As I got into my car, my phone rang, and Derrick's picture flashed on the screen. Activating the blue tooth in my car for hands-free usage, I answered.

Before I could say anything, I heard the sweet voice of a child. "Mary Jane, I wanted to call and tell you good night before Daddy talks to you. And thank you for my gifts. I'm glad you two are still friends. Not just because I get presents though."

As a grin stretched across my face, warm comfort soothed me. My night with Tristan had been a lot of fun, but talking to Katelyn and Derrick was my favorite thing to do. "Hey, Katie-cat! I miss you, sweetie."

She sighed dramatically. "Me too. Daddy says you work at Disney World. Can I come out there and go on rides with you?"

I giggled as I heard Derrick in the background say, "She doesn't ride rides all day long, Katie."

Katelyn scoffed. "I know, Daddy. I meant she could do that on her day off with me." She came back to the phone and said, "Men."

The tone of voice she used when uttering that one word caused me to break into a small fit of laughter. "Who taught you that? Uncle Cameron?" Katie giggled, letting me know that was indeed her teacher.

Derrick again piped up. "You need to spend a little less time with Uncle Cam, I think. Say goodnight, Katelyn. You have pre-school in the morning."

Katelyn giggled again. "Goodnight, Katelyn. And goodnight, MJ, I love you."

Those words always made me smile when she said them. "I love you too, Katie-cat. Sweet dreams."

Derrick took the phone and sighed. "What am I going to do with that girl?"

I responded, "What would you do without her?"

He chuckled. "Touché." Then he asked, "Where are my manners? Hello, beautiful, how was your day?" This man could make my heart swell to the point of bursting with his sweet words. And to think, I almost missed out on this due to a few hundred miles between us.

"It was good. It's even better now that I'm talking to you."

I could hear the smile in his voice as he asked, "So, what did you do?"

"I met someone." His silence spoke volumes about the assumption he made. "Oh wait, no, not a guy. I mean it's a guy, but he's a friend."

He must have been holding his breath because I heard a long exhale of breath before he said, "Don't give a guy a heart attack like that, sweetheart."

It made me a little happy he was worried about it, even daresay… jealous. "You have nothing to worry about, believe me. Though technically, a guy did ask for my number."

Acting as though he was frustrated, he said, "That's it. I'm on my way down there now."

All I could do was laugh at his adorable jealous act.

"The guy I hung out with tonight, his name is Tristan. He's incredibly sweet. You'd like him." For the next few minutes, I occupied the conversation by telling him all about the luau.

When I told him about Macy, I heard the emotion in his voice when he said, "I worry about Katelyn being bullied. I'm not sure what I'd do in that situation." The very idea made my blood boil. I imagined for Derrick it was a more intense emotion. Derrick put Katelyn above everyone in his life, as it should be with a child.

"Well, you wouldn't have to do anything because I'd kick anyone's butt who hurts that little girl. No matter what consequences I faced." No truer words had been spoken. In the short time I'd known them both, I'd fallen hard for Derrick and Katelyn. Every decision I made, I took the two of them into consideration first.

He laughed softly. "I miss you, sweetheart."

I choked back tears at those words. "I miss you too." Wiping my eyes, I put the car in Park and sighed. "I'm home for the evening. I'll call you tomorrow if you're free?"

"I'm always available for you. Sweet dreams tonight." Nights spent talking to him always ended in the sweetest, and sometimes dirtiest, dreams.

Chapter Six

DERRICK

Mary Jane and I had been talking back and forth for almost five months without anyone finding out. Then one day, I called Cameron to talk to him about a business idea, and he said he didn't have time to talk because he was packing for Florida.

"Wait, what? Are you going to Florida? For what?" I asked.

"I'm headed down to spend time with my girl, MJ. Ooh… sorry, Derrick, I wasn't thinking about who I'm talking to." Cameron's voice became awkward as he fumbled to change the subject.

"It's cool, Cam. Um… can you keep a secret?" It allowed for a perfect opportunity for me to send something to Mary Jane. Cameron probably wasn't the best person to trust with a secret, but I had to hope that he'd come through for me.

"Does my ass look great in everything?" he responded.

"Is that a question or answer?" I asked, confused.

"Both. So spill already!" Practically able to hear him bouncing up and down with excitement at finding out a secret, I didn't make him wait any longer.

"Would you stop by before you leave town. I have something for MJ. We've kind of been seeing each other long distance. We don't want to tell anyone though, in case it ends up not working out."

"Shut the front door! I knew it! I told everyone that I figured you two were bumping on the side and leaving us out of the juicy details!" he exclaimed excitedly.

"There hasn't been any bumping. We've been Skyping and talking on the phone."

Cameron made a "pshh" sound. "No bumping? Derrick, baby, that is not a CamWow secret."

"CamWow?" I asked again, perplexed.

"Yep, you have to be able to wow the Cam with your secrets, and I'm not feeling the wow. I feel very disappointed. Do me a favor, once the bumping in secret starts, fill me in, please? But yes, I'll deliver your package." He snickered for a moment and said, "Although I'm sure she'd rather you give a different package in person."

"Thanks, Cameron. I'll see you shortly." I hung up before the conversation took an even more awkward turn. Cameron was a bit over the top, but he meant well, though somehow he had the talent to turn the most innocent phrase into something sexual.

An hour later, Cameron knocked on the door. I opened it to find him leaning against the frame. He lowered his sunglasses and winked. "Hey there, hot stuff, I came to grab your package."

Shaking my head, I waved him inside. "Give me a sec, and I'll grab it for you."

"Whew! Honey, I am a married man. You can't talk about stuff like that around me!" Cameron said, fanning himself.

Taking the steps two at a time, I ran to my room to get the gift for Mary Jane. When I came back downstairs, I handed it to Cameron, who stared at it a moment before asking, "Can I look at it since I'm playing delivery boy?"

"Sure," I said, opening the box for him. Inside was a silver locket with a photo of Katelyn on one side and a photo of me on the other. "I thought it would be a way for us to be with her. Is it cheesy?"

"Yeah, a little, but romantic gestures usually are cheesy. I love it, and I know she will too. I'm rooting for you guys, Derrick. I truly am." Cameron pulled me close for a hug, patting my back before letting me go again.

"Thanks, man, I appreciate it. Remember, don't tell anyone about us, please. We want to see how this works without any interference or upsetting Katelyn."

He nodded, then took his index finger and made an X over his heart. "Cross my heart."

After Cameron left, I ran errands for the day. My first stop was my brother Ashton's house. Ashton and Gracie had a baby on the way after only five months of wedded bliss.

Before I could knock on the door, it swung open, and

Gracie jumped back with a squeak of surprise. "Derrick! You about gave me a heart attack."

Ashton came running around the corner. "Gracie!" Even though the threat of her stalker was gone, Ashton still jumped anytime Gracie sounded scared. "Shit, bro, why didn't you call first?"

Instinctively, I lifted my hand to cover my eyes. "Wow, I really wish I had now." When I said Ashton came running around the corner, well, he was completely naked at the time.

Gracie shrugged, glancing over at Ashton as he turned to go back to their room. "You couldn't have gotten a better view if you ask me." She laughed and waved me inside. "Take a seat. I was on my way out to run some errands for school supplies. It can wait though. I never get to visit with my favorite brother-in-law. You want something to drink?" Gracie was still in college, working to get her degree in psychology.

"A Coke would be nice, thanks, Gracie." Their house was always spotless. At one time, the walls displayed paintings of scenery Ashton had drawn, but they were replaced with pictures of their wedding and their life in general. The only painting still on the wall consisted of one Ashton did of their wedding photo. All his other paintings went into the man cave, his basement rec room.

"Here you are," Gracie said, handing me the canned drink. "How've you been?" she asked, meaning she wanted to know how I was coping with losing Mary Jane. My sister-in-law was easy to read, even when she was trying to be subtle.

"Good. How's MJ?" It felt silly asking since I talked to Mary Jane every day; but if we were going to keep this relationship a secret, then I had to be careful not to cause suspicion. Truthfully, I wanted to confess everything to Gracie. The only thing keeping me from doing it was it could get back to Katelyn, and I needed to protect my daughter in case things didn't go the way I wanted them to.

She grinned. "Was it that obvious of a question? Sorry. She's good too, I think. She and Angel seem to like their new place. Cameron's on his way down today to spend some time with them. I wanted to go, but school got in the way. I'm going to make a trip before I get too far along to fly though." She rubbed her nonexistent belly as she talked about the baby on the way.

"Katelyn's going to be so excited to have a cousin. She hoped they'd have birthdays in the same month, but I had to break it to her that you were only a little over a month along so it would be September, not June, before the baby comes." Adjusting the subject away from Mary Jane seemed the best idea to keep me from saying the wrong thing. At that moment, Ashton returned to the room fully dressed. "Glad you could join us in clothes this time."

Ashton leaned down and kissed Gracie's head. "Hello, my beautiful wife" —And then he leaned over to kiss her stomach— "and my beautiful baby."

Gracie giggled at his greeting, giving him a soft kiss once his face came back up to hers again. "I'll leave you two to talk. I'll be back in a bit." Ashton and I stood with her, as good gentlemen do. Gracie gave me a hug and whispered, "Call MJ. I know she'd love to hear from you. I'm still rooting for you guys."

After she had left, I told Ashton, "That girl there is awesome."

"You don't have to tell me. Why do you think I married her?" Ashton led the way down to his man cave so we could talk. "So, what's the idea you wanted to run by me?"

"Remember when we were younger and talked about running our own club one day?" Ashton nodded, so I continued. "What's wrong with now? Cameron is graduating with his interior design degree, Gavin negotiates commercial real estate, you have the contacts for entertainment, and I have the security contacts. We have the perfect arrangement. The four of us can run it together, as a family."

With his thumb and index finger, Ashton rubbed at his beard, his eyes squinted in thought. I could see the wheels turning as he ran over all the details in his mind. When a smile formed on his face, he said, "I love it. Let's do this."

We worked for hours mapping out details of what we wanted to do with our nightclub. By the end of the day, we had chosen a general locale to look for a building, the first entertainment we'd want for the opening week, and the type of menu that would be popular, other than alcoholic drinks of course.

We were getting things on track, and I had something to lose myself in, instead of moping about missing Mary Jane.

My phone had gone off several times while we were meeting. Each time, I checked it to be sure it wasn't Katelyn. Three of the missed texts were from Mary Jane. Reading the first one made me smile.

Mary Jane: I love my locket; it's the best gift I've received since the mug you gave me the day I moved. You're amazing.

With the second text, my smile grew larger.

Mary Jane: My friend Tristan and I are taking Cameron out tonight. It may be late when we get home, but I'd love to talk if you feel up to it. I miss you.

And text three made me chuckle.

Mary Jane: Forgot to say, text me when you go to bed if you haven't heard from me. That way I know it's too late to call.

Even if I didn't get a wink of sleep, I wasn't going to tell her it would be too late to call me. I wanted, no needed, to hear her sweet voice. I needed to tell her the news about the nightclub.

Me: Definitely text me tonight. I want to talk to you. I miss your voice, and it helps me sleep after hearing it.

CHAPTER SEVEN

MARY JANE

"Where is this hot studly friend you told me about, MJ?" Cameron asked the moment we arrived at my apartment.

"He's performing tonight, and then we're all going out afterward."

"Performing? Is that a subtle way of saying he's getting freaky?" Cameron wiggled his eyebrows.

"Is everything about sex with you? Never mind, stupid question. He's filling in one of the dance numbers for a coworker at the park."

He clapped his hands excitedly. "Let's go watch! I love dance numbers!"

"Really? Okay, let me change and grab my badge to get us in free." Slipping on some comfy jeans, a black tank top with sparkles, and some of my best cowboy boots from back home, I glanced in the mirror to check myself out. Since I'd moved to Florida, between the sweating and extra walking, I'd lost about twenty pounds.

Cameron whistled when I walked out of the bedroom. "Baby girl, you look amazing. Love sure does look good on you."

"Love? No, Tristan and I are simply good friends."

"Not Tristan. I know about you and Derrick. In fact, he asked me to give you this," he said as he reached into his pocket and pulled out a small jewelry box. Inside was a beautiful silver locket. As I opened it to see the pictures inside, I became teary.

"Aww, baby girl, you do love him, don't you?" Though all I could do was nod, Cameron was elated by my response. Bouncing and clapping his hands, he exclaimed, "This is so awesome! We're all going to be a real family soon. Since Gavin is his adopted brother, you, Gracie, and I will have landed a set of brothers! Now they need to scrounge up one more for Angel and life would be perfect."

"Don't get ahead of yourself, Cameron. The relationship is still new for us, and there is a lot to work around. We live hundreds of miles away from each other, and the successfulness of long-distance relationships is not high."

"Don't think so negatively, sweets," Cameron said, disappointed in my pessimism.

"I don't mean to be negative. I'm realistic is all. So far, things are amazing, so I'm hopeful." Cameron took the hint and dropped the subject.

We went to see Tristan perform, and both thought the

show was fantastic. It was the first time I'd seen Tristan dance. He had a lot of rhythm and a great singing voice too. Afterward, I sent Tristan a text to meet at my apartment before we went out.

We'd been home for a few minutes when we heard a knock on the door. "I'll get it!" Cameron yelled out. "Hot damn! Hello, you must be Tristud."

Tristan laughed and held his hand out. "It's Tristan."

"Nope, I had it right the first time," Cameron said, flirting.

"You have to be Cameron. You're exactly as MJ described you." Tristan walked into the room while Cameron shut the door behind him.

"Sexy, funny, perfect in every way, a package of awesome… that's her description, right? It's all true. I won't deny it."

"I see you've met Cameron and his ego," I said, walking in to greet Tristan.

Tristan lifted me up in a bear hug. "He's great. I could totally hang with this guy." He glanced around the room. "Where's Angel tonight?"

"Working late again. She had to take on an extra half shift to cover one of the girls who called in. I know she hates missing Cameron here." Working as a bartender wasn't Angel's dream job, but the tips helped tremendously with our bills. The downside was it meant we rarely saw each other since my schedule changed week to week and she worked mostly nights.

"What did you guys think of the show tonight?"

"Well, you're no Johnny Castle," Cam said.

"Who is Johnny Castle?" Tristan asked.

"*Dirty Dancing*? Patrick Swayze? Ring a bell now?" Cam asked.

Tristan replied, "Nope, never seen the movie." And as soon as he said those words, I knew it was going to be a long night. Cue the drama from Cameron.

Cameron's mouth dropped open in shock. "Get out."

Tristan chuckled. "I'm serious. I've never seen it." A loud smack was the only sound in the room for a moment as my palm slammed against my forehead at Tristan's mistake in admitting such a travesty in Cameron's eyes.

Cameron pointed at the door. "No, seriously, get out! No one is allowed in my presence if they haven't seen *Dirty Dancing*! 'Nobody puts Baby in a corner' either!" In an overly dramatic display only Cameron could get away with, he stormed off to my bedroom, slamming the door closed behind him.

Tristan, startled at the sound of the door, turned to me. "Is he serious?"

"Cameron is serious about his movies. He's one of the most awesome friends anyone could ask for though, which is how he gets away with that stuff. You've seen *The Breakfast Club* though, right?"

Tristan shook his head. I wrapped my arm through his and sighed. "Sheesh, man. We're having a movie night tonight. If he finds out you don't know who John Bender is, you'll never pass his approval to be in the group."

"Wait, what about Macy?" I had forgotten Tristan had

responsibilities at home.

"She is staying with a neighbor who has a daughter the same age. She covers for me when I have to work late. It's her first time having a sleepover." Tristan had a pensive look on his face. "I know Judd Nelson, Anthony Michael Hall, and Emilio Estevez are in it, but I don't remember anyone named John Bender though. Is he still acting?"

I rolled my eyes and pressed my hand over his mouth. "Stop talking, Tristan, you're digging yourself a deeper grave here." There was a reason we called Cameron a drama queen, but he said he was a drama princess because his mother was still alive.

When Cameron heard the music for *Dirty Dancing* starting, he ran into the room and plopped onto the couch between us. Every scene where they were dancing, Cameron got up to mimic the moves and tried desperately to get one of us to dance with him. I finally agreed to do a little of the end number with him, minus the lift.

We put *The Breakfast Club* in and settled down for a more relaxed movie. After a night of catching Tristan up on the movies he missed, he decided to crash on the couch instead of driving home. Cameron was still wide awake and bouncing in his seat. The energy level on this man rivaled a toddler most days. "What do you want to do now?" The man could run for three days straight with no rest and still be perky.

Glancing at my watch, I saw it was well after midnight in Nashville. I checked my phone, and there were no texts from Derrick about him going to sleep.

"Can we call it a night? I want to call Derrick before I go to bed."

Cameron stood up, grabbed a beer from the fridge, and waved to me. "I'm crashing in Angel's room. She won't mind, she'll snuggle with me when she gets home. I'm going to call my man too. Tomorrow, you and me, babe, right?"

"Absolutely. We're spending the entire day together tomorrow. We'll do anything you want to do," I said. Cameron winked at me, then shut the door to Angel's room. Grabbing a blanket from the couch, I tossed it over Tristan before going to my room.

Me: Skype or phone?

Derrick: Skype, I need to see that beautiful face.

Excitedly, I logged on to my laptop. The cursor rotated for what seemed like forever before the connection completed. His handsome face was there on the screen for me when I opened it. I gulped. "You're not wearing a shirt." All I wanted to do was run my fingers across his sculpted chest.

He glanced down. "If it makes you uncomfortable, I can put one on, or you can take yours off too." I found myself unable to respond, still mesmerized by his muscular form. A smirk came across his face. "Sweetheart, I miss you so much."

"Me too," I finally managed to say. I fingered the necklace he gave me. "I love this, by the way." Wearing the two of them so close to my heart made me feel like we were a family.

"I'm glad." He didn't say anything else for a moment. "I

want to see you. I'm going to figure out a way and soon."

"I'd love it. Just let me know when. I won't have more than a day or two off for a while, or I'd come there to you." My door creaked open, and Cameron peaked inside. "Hold on, Derrick. Cameron, are you okay?" He shook his head, and I turned back to Derrick. "Can we talk tomorrow? Cameron needs my attention."

"Absolutely." Then, he yelled out, "Thanks, Cameron, for delivering my package, man."

"No problem." Cameron didn't even comment on the word package or make any crude jokes, which told me something was very wrong with him.

The call ended. I closed my laptop and lifted my comforter from the empty side of the bed. "Come snuggle, Cam." Cameron moped over to the vacant side of the bed, slid in, and curled up against me with his head against my chest. "What's wrong, sweetie?"

"Everything," he mumbled with not even an ounce of energy behind it. Now I began to worry this would be a cheering up job bigger than I could handle.

"What happened to the happy Cameron who went off to talk to his man? Did you have a fight with Gavin?" That was the first thought I had since he was supposed to be on the phone with him at that moment, but it seemed odd to even ask because the two of them never so much as spat over little things, let alone have full-blown arguments.

"No, my husband is as fabulous as ever. It seems nothing fazes him, which is great because he keeps me grounded." Cameron scooted in closer to me as I began to scratch his back.

"So then why the sad face?" Cameron, always our comic relief, was displaying unusual behavior as he stared forward in silence with his eyes glazed over.

Sitting up, he fidgeted with the comforter as he collected his thoughts. "I'm tired of having to defend who I am. It's exhausting, and it's unfair. It's also tiring to pretend not to have a care in the world."

"What do you mean?" I asked, taking one of his hands in mine. Stroking his palm, I watched his face as the emotions warred with each other.

"I'm gay, Mary Jane."

Attempting to make him laugh, I gasped dramatically. "What! No! It can't be true!" He gave my shoulder a little shove with a light chuckle, but it wasn't the response I wanted. "I'm sorry. I was trying to make you laugh."

"I love you for it, sweetie. What I mean is, I'm tired of my whole life being condensed to the fact I'm gay. You and Derrick could go get married right now, and no one would give you any grief. You could kiss in the middle of a park filled with people, and they would think it was sweet and romantic. I hold Gavin's hand and get looks of disgust from people I've never spoken to." Cameron took a deep breath to hold back the tears I could tell were about to fall.

Cameron and Gavin deserved their happily ever after more than anyone I knew. Both men put others before themselves, were loyal to their friends and family, and never did anything to intentionally hurt anyone. "You and Gavin are one of the most loving couples I've ever witnessed.

You're perfect for each other, and while I know it doesn't make it easier, you have to forget what those few people think."

"We've been looking to adopt. You're the first one to know. I haven't even told Gracie. It's one of the reasons I wanted to visit. I needed a break from the stress of it all. Gavin thought it would be difficult to be sad here of all places." The fact he hadn't said anything to Gracie was shocking to me. Cameron and Gracie had been best friends since they were five. If Cameron wasn't gay, I had no doubt they'd have gotten married by now. They told each other everything.

"What? That's wonderful news! You and Gavin will make fabulous parents," I exclaimed, truly ecstatic. Cameron would be a fantastic father. He was practically a big kid himself. Katelyn adored him, though Derrick wished sometimes she didn't try to emulate him so much.

"You'd think so. We've made appointments, and each time we show up, they are surprised I'm a male named Cameron, the rest of the appointment becomes an awkward conversation about the difficulty of adopting because there is so much demand. In truth, it's difficult because we're two men. Some of them came right out and said that to us, which was better than the runaround. You can't imagine how hard it is to defend your love to everyone."

It was true. I couldn't relate, but it didn't mean my heart wasn't breaking for him though. If Derrick proposed to me, no one would say a negative word about it. We'd have no problems getting a marriage license; we'd be ideal adoptive parents, and we'd never have to fight for the state to admit our marriage was real.

Suddenly, my thoughts were blank; I couldn't come up with anything to make this better for him. What could I as a straight woman offer as solace to my friend? I couldn't understand his pain, but I wanted to do anything I could to ease it. "Cameron, I love you." My tears fell as I spoke the only thing I could that was absolute truth and not just a hopeful anecdote. Understanding the deeper meaning behind my words, he wrapped his arms around neck as we sobbed together.

Cameron sat up first. He grasped my face in his hands. "Look at me." My eyes met his, and he said, "You are one very sexy woman. You are desirable. You're sweet, and you have the biggest heart of anyone I've ever known. Never forget that."

"You never let me, and for that I adore you. You always put your friends' happiness above your own, and that's why you've been our group hero. But tonight is about cheering you up. You're the number one priority" My laptop was still beside the bed. I shifted my body to set it on my lap. "We're going to do some research. There must be a way you can adopt. Maybe international is the way to go. Whatever it takes, we're going to go over every possibility."

Cameron pointed at the clock. "It's after 2:00 a.m."

"Doesn't matter. We're going to make you a daddy in this bed tonight."

He wiggled his eyebrows at me. "I'm a married man, you naughty girl."

CHAPTER EIGHT

DERRICK

The last few nights, my conversations with Mary Jane had been through text only. She'd wanted to spend as much time with Cameron as possible. Though I missed our chats, I couldn't fault her for it. Therefore, when my phone rang, flashing her beautiful face, I had to excuse myself without too many questions arising since I was at Ashton's at the time. "Um… I gotta take this. It's important." I ran out of the room, up the stairs, and out the front door with Gracie calling out, asking me where the fire was. "MJ?"

"Hey, Derrick. Sorry, it's been a little while."

"Too long. I missed hearing your voice." She grew quiet, and I tried to back out of the insecure moment. "Is everything okay?"

"I'm fine. I called because I missed your voice too.

That's not true. I called because I miss everything about you." Hearing those sweet words, I wanted to wrap my arms around her. That need was hindered due to a few hundred miles between us.

"I miss you too, sweetheart." Simple words sounded petty in comparison to the immense loneliness I suffered without her.

"Can you take a few days off work and come see me this weekend? I'll meet you halfway, maybe even as far as Atlanta? I have this weekend off, and I'd love to spend it with you, if you can manage it." Images of the two of us alone in a hotel room played through my mind.

As soon as she finished speaking, I answered, "Absolutely. Tell me when and where." Well, that didn't make me seem desperate at all. Then again, it didn't matter if I seemed desperate; I craved this woman and needed to see her.

"Oh… great. I wasn't sure you were going to want to come see me."

"MJ, I meant what I said. I've missed you. Not just your voice. I've missed your beautiful face, your lips, and the feel of you in my arms." I stopped as I realized I hadn't asked if she meant to spend it as friends or more. I was met with silence. "Damn, MJ. Did you want me to come down as a friend only? I didn't mean to push for anything else."

She laughed, and I relaxed as she said, "I want you, Derrick. Not as a friend. I want to be in your arms again, and I want to kiss you and… other things."

Her voice lowered to a sexy whisper, and if she'd been

in front of me right then, I'd have shown her how it affected me. "Oh" was all I could manage. She responded with a laugh, and I closed my eyes as I ached for her. "MJ, I gotta get off here."

She purred and said, "I was hoping you'd wait for me."

Now I had to walk back into Gracie and Ashton's house sporting wood after telling them I was taking a business call.

"Shit, MJ, you're killing me." Nine months ago, when we met, she was so shy. I wondered what else about her could have changed since she moved. Not that I was complaining, I loved the open Mary Jane as well, but I didn't want her to change so much we no longer fit together.

"Sorry, I couldn't help myself. You left that wide open for me." Another sexy giggle from her and I would've had to go home and call my brother to say goodbye.

We made plans to meet in Atlanta so we could do some sightseeing and enjoy our few days together. Gracie and Ashton agreed to keep Katelyn for me. Katelyn thought I was going on a trip for work, because if she knew I was going to see Mary Jane, she'd want to come along.

The week crept on as my anxiety for the weekend heightened. Midway through, I went to pick up some supplies for my trip. I grabbed the normal toiletries and a few snacks for the road so I could make as few stops as possible. My peripheral vision caught the display of condoms as I left the aisle. I wasn't sure if it seemed presumptuous or responsible to grab a pack for the trip. I was going with responsible, which was appropriate for me being a father as a teenager.

"Derrick?" I heard Gracie's voice call out as I rounded

the corner to the next aisle. "Are you stocking up on supplies for your trip?" She maintained a warm smile until her eyes skimmed over the condoms package. "Oh." *Dammit.*

"It's not what it looks like, Gracie." Well, there was a cliché that never worked out when delivered because it was almost always exactly as it appeared.

"It looks like you're buying a pack of condoms for the trip you said was for business. What kind of business are you conducting exactly?" She placed her hand on her hip for a moment, then waved it in the air. "Forget it, I don't want to know. We'll see you and Katelyn in the morning." Though I knew the truth, I couldn't allow Gracie to think I was betraying Mary Jane.

"Gracie, wait," I yelled out. She turned around but avoided eye contact with me. I moved my cart to her and said, "I've been lying to you, to Ash, to everyone about where I'm going and who I'm seeing."

Gracie interrupted before I got to my point. "It's not my business, Derrick. Do I wish you had worked things out with MJ? Yes, I do. You two were great together, but she told me that she told you to move on. If that's what you're doing, then I know it's what MJ wanted for you."

"Gracie, I'm doing this for MJ," I said.

Again, she interrupted. "I get it, I do."

"No, you don't. When I say I'm doing this for MJ, I mean the trip and all. She and I have been talking for months. She asked me to meet her in Atlanta this weekend. We didn't want to tell anyone because of the chance we couldn't work it out. Neither of us wanted to lie to you guys, but…"

Gracie crashed into me with enormous force for such a small girl. She wrapped her arms around my neck in a tight hug. "I'm so happy for you guys." She pulled back suddenly, and said, "Wait, have you two… I mean… MJ is…" She didn't seem able to finish her sentence as she kept glancing at the box of condoms. It occurred to me what she was asking.

"I know that she's never. She made it sound like she wants to this weekend. I only want to be prepared. I'd never push her into that decision though."

Gracie smiled. "I know you wouldn't. It's why I'm so happy she has you. She needs a guy with a heart like Ash's, and no one's is closer than yours."

"Thanks, Gracie. That means a lot to me." My phone beeped, and it was a text from Mary Jane. I held my phone up to show her. "See. She's telling me she can't wait to see me this weekend."

Gracie squealed, bounced up and down, and clapped her hands. "I won't tell anyone, except Ashton of course. I don't keep secrets from him."

"That's fine. Cameron knows too actually."

Her mouth opened in shock, and she exclaimed, "What! Big mouth Cam knows, and you didn't think you could trust us not to tell?"

"You have a point. I didn't mean for him to find out, but I needed him to deliver something to MJ for me when he went to see her, so I filled him in." It surprised me Cameron hadn't told Gracie already. I needed to commend him on his ability to keep a secret.

After leaving the grocery store, I sped home to finish packing. In two days, I'd be on my way to Atlanta. The four-hour drive to see her was going to feel like the longest one of my life. It already felt as though time slowed since we made plans to meet.

When the day arrived to leave, I couldn't stop my hands from shaking or my stomach from twisting with nerves. Katelyn had her bag packed and was in her room waiting for me to come get her. "Hey, baby girl, you ready to spend a few days with Aunt Gracie and Uncle Ash?"

Elated, she jumped up from her chair. "Yes! Can I take the new movie MJ sent me?" All the gifts Mary Jane sent her become her favorite of the week. The movie came in last week, and already she'd watched it ten times. I thought I'd go crazy from singing the songs continuously in my mind.

"Sure. You know your uncle will watch anything you want. You've got him whipped." It was true. If Katelyn said she wanted a pony, Ashton would get her one. No wasn't in his vocabulary when she was around.

"What's whipped mean?" Katelyn asked.

"Never mind. Grab your bag and let's go."

Katelyn liked to carry her bags to feel like a big girl, so I bought her a wheeled suitcase that was small enough to not be too bulky for her. Cartoon skulls with pink bows on them covered the black fabric bag. She picked it out, but I had to admit it was cool. She clomped down the stairs with the bag banging on each step behind her. She stopped midway and sneezed three times in a row.

"Hey, kiddo, you're not getting sick, are you?"

"Nah, I feel fine," Katelyn responded. She reached the bottom of the stairs and stepped outside so I could turn on the alarm, then lock the house down. On the way to Ashton and Gracie's, she sneezed a few more times, making me a little nervous. Knowing how overprotective I was, she reassured me before I even asked the question. "I'm fine, Daddy. Something's tickling my nose."

"I can stay home, boo," I said. "Your Aunt Gracie is pregnant and doesn't need to get sick."

"Daddy, it's fine," she said. I spotted her in the rearview mirror rolling her eyes at me. "My nose doesn't even feel stuffy."

Playing it safe, I picked up a few supplies at the local pharmacy in case she did have a small cold beginning. When we arrived at Ashton's house, he was standing outside watching for us. "What happened to you being here at 8:00 a.m. sharp? You drilled that into my head several times as I recall." Ashton was smirking at me, knowing how finicky I was about my schedules. I had called him at least four times, reiterating eight in the morning because I knew he and Gracie liked to sleep in, and I wanted to make sure everyone was decent when I showed up with my daughter in tow.

"Hey, boo!" Ashton said, grabbing Katelyn and spinning her around. "You ready for a weekend of fun?"

"Be careful with her there, Ash. We're running late because I had to stop and get a few medicines. She promises me she feels fine, but she's been sneezing."

Ashton gasps dramatically. "What? Sneezing? Oh my gosh, what will we do?" He and Katelyn both laughed at my expense.

"I told him to chill, Uncle Ash. He never listens to me," Katelyn said, again rolling her eyes.

"Look here, little girl, you keep rolling your eyes like that, and they're going to stick that way." I reached up and tickled her, then gave her a kiss on the cheek. "I love you, boo. You be good for your aunt and uncle."

"Katie, go inside and help your Aunt Gracie finish breakfast." Once her feet hit the ground, Katelyn sprinted away to the kitchen. Ashton's body twisted back to face me as he smirked. "So, MJ? You sneaky devil." Big brothers had a real knack for giving their younger siblings a hard time. My big brother had more tact than most. "Seriously, man, I'm happy for you. Now get out of here and have a safe trip."

Before I turned to leave, I sent him a text. "I'm texting you the number for Katelyn's pediatrician in case this is a cold or something more. Any money you spend, I promise to pay back."

Ashton grasped my shoulders to make me look up. "She's fine. Go and see your woman. Stop worrying so much about everything. Gracie and I will take care of Katie."

"Thanks again, man." With a quick hug, I slipped behind the wheel and drove off, reminding myself Katelyn was in the best hands possible, other than mine.

The golden gas pump light glowed brightly on my dash,

alerting me it was time to make a stop. As the gasoline flowed furiously into my tank, I stepped aside to text Mary Jane.

Me: Hey, sweetheart. Stopped for gas. I'm about 20 minutes away. See you soon.

Before getting back on the road, I ran inside to pick up another important thing for the trip. Timing had worked out to have our weekend only a week before Valentine's day. I'd given MJ the locket, but I wanted to have something in hand tonight when I saw her. The clerk behind the counter mindlessly flipped through her magazine of gossip news while popping her gum. She grunted when I asked, "Do you have any flowers?" She nodded toward the left of the register, and I noticed a vase of red roses packaged in singles. "Great, I'll take one of those, please." The register spat out my change, and she went back to reading her magazine. "Have a great night!" I added, hoping to elicit a response. Nothing. Customer service these days was nonexistent.

Checking my phone before driving off, I saw that Mary Jane had responded.

Mary Jane: Can't wait to see you. I'm checked into the hotel. When you get here, check in, and they'll give you a key to our room.

I hadn't felt this nervous about sharing a room with someone, well, ever. It felt like my first time again. Nerves ate away at me, and I expected the drive to be longer because of them. The vibrant green sign alerted me of the exit ahead for Atlanta. My clammy palms gripped the steering wheel as my stomach churned with nervous excitement.

Not far off the interstate, I found the hotel we'd decided on. Spotting Mary Jane's car, I swallowed back the anxiety and took the spot across from her. Starting my way inside, I had to turn back for a moment when I realized I'd left my luggage in the car.

Finally through the entry, I walked up to the counter and found the desk clerk was a bit friendlier than the one at the gas station. Politely, I smiled and told her to have a good weekend before pressing the Up arrow on the side of the elevator door.

CHAPTER NINE

MARY JANE

Derrick had agreed to meet me in Atlanta without even thinking about it. From the moment he said yes, the days crept by, making my nerves heighten dramatically.

Because more of our friends were finding out the truth, I confided in Angel. When I told her about my plan, she decided to help me make it even more memorable. Angel and Gracie were more experienced in life than I was. I'd always been a plus-sized woman and had issues with feeling insecure about my weight, so much so I didn't trust men were truly attracted to me. I was about to make some changes in my life, and the first thing I needed to do was make sure my first time was with someone I loved. Everything about the timing seemed right. We had been flirting with the idea for weeks with subtle innuendo, and sometimes it wasn't so subtle.

Once I arrived in Atlanta, I settled into the swanky hotel room I splurged on and began the meticulous task of unpacking my duffel bag. My phone dinged alerting me to a new text. Derrick had just gotten off the interstate for gas and would be here in about twenty minutes.

Angel packed me a surprise and made me promise I wouldn't peek until I was at the hotel. It was a pristine white box with a velvet red bow draped beautifully around it. I tore into it, anxious to see the surprise that awaited me. Inside was a sheer robe with a silk nightgown, white as snow, underneath. The note read, "Wear this for your first time." Underneath the negligee was a knock-your-man-off-his-feet-sexy, deep crimson, all-lace bra and panty set with garters and thigh highs with another note. "Wear this for your second time." I'm sure my skin was a deeper shade of crimson than the lingerie I held in my hands. At least the first one was elegant looking, that I would have no problem wearing.

Derrick would arrive any minute, so I had a short time to prepare his surprise. My toes curled against the supple carpet as I made my way barefoot into the restroom to change. Undressing quickly, I jumped into the shower to shave my legs and freshen up everything. Inhaling the scent of the new strawberry and mint body wash I'd bought, I hoped he'd like the smell of it on my skin.

Stepping out, I wrapped a towel around my body and used another to dry my hair, leaving it wavy and damp. Letting the towel drop to the floor I slid the silk nightgown over my head, wincing as the cool material fell against my skin, making my nipples peak. With a deep breath for courage, I slid the robe on, not sure why it was necessary since it was so sheer, but it made me feel less exposed.

Derrick's voice called out, "MJ? Are you here, sweetheart?" Listening as the door shut, I waited to call out to him. Knees weak, I reached to steady myself on the counter.

"Be right out," I called. Suddenly, I was terribly nervous, and I wanted to crawl back into the clothes I had on before. Knowing my nerves would get the best of me, I'd tossed my clothes back into the room before I had changed so I couldn't chicken out. Regret over that decision was abundant at that moment.

Stepping out into the room, I bit my lip when I saw Derrick with his back to me. The sharp, woody scent of his cologne wafted into my nose, causing my legs to quiver as my need to touch him grew stronger. I took a few steps closer to him before saying, "Hey there, stranger." As he turned, his smile suddenly dropped into a shocked expression. "Does this look bad?" I asked. It was hard to decipher if his reaction was good or bad.

Slowly shaking his head back and forth, he closed the space between us with two broad steps. "You're the most beautiful woman I've ever seen." His lips found mine before I could respond to his sweet compliment. Our passion exploded, filling us with need, desire, and love. His strong hands gently cradled my face as his lips ravaged mine. His palms drifted to my shoulders, and his lips trailed across my skin. As his tongue drew circles across my neck, tasting every inch, I let out a soft moan.

Pausing briefly, he asked, "Are you sure this is what you want?" My ability to speak was completely gone; I could only nod. "There's something I need to tell you before we do this."

My stomach tightened. What kind of confession could he have at this moment? Did he have a girlfriend now? Had he slept with someone recently? Did he have a disease? The possibilities were endless. "What is it?" I asked, fearful of the answer.

His index finger traced lines across my cheek. Leaning down, he brushed his lips against mine once more, following it with a smile. "Before we do this, before you give yourself to me, I need you to know something. I'm not saying this to get in your pants either. You deserve to know how I feel about you and what this will mean to me. You're amazing, Mary Jane. The most amazing woman I've ever known. Since the moment I met you, I haven't wanted anything else but to be with you completely. Even if you decide after this you don't want a relationship or you want to wait till your internship is completed, you need to know one thing. I love you."

A confession of love wasn't what I expected at all. "I love you, so much, Derrick." In reality, I'd known I was in love with Derrick for a while. Neither of us had come right out and said it, which left me worried he may not feel the same.

Derrick's broad smile brightened the room. His arms

enveloped me, lifting me off the floor, as he kissed me fiercely. When he sat me down, he pushed the robe off my shoulders, replacing it with his mouth. His tongue tasted my skin as it explored my collarbone. I tugged his belt, luring him toward the bed. Falling back against the soft mattress, I opened my legs and pulled Derrick close to me. His pale blue polo shirt kept me from tasting his skin. Tugging it free from his pants, I lifted it and made my way across his chiseled abs with my lips, darting my tongue out to savor the flavor of his body.

His leather belt slid easily through his belt loops. I unfastened the top button of his pants and pressed my lips to the soft line of hair leading down to his happy place. Evidence of his excitement pressed against his boxer briefs, and he groaned as my hand grazed his erection. Quickly, he stood to remove his shirt completely before rejoining me on the bed, this time hovering above me. His hand slid up my thigh, his fingers tickling my skin as they traveled further north. His mouth found mine, and our tongues danced together. Derrick's fingers traced the hem of my lingerie to discover the other surprise awaiting him.

"No panties? Damn, MJ, I want you." He growled seductively.

Derrick moved down the bed, and. I shivered as his lips moved up the inside of my thigh. When he reached my core, I arched my back from the most intense pleasure I'd ever experienced. My fantasies couldn't touch the reality of the moment.

Derrick pushed the silk negligee up and pulled it over

my head. His mouth instantly found my nipple. I moaned and breathily said, "Wait, let me… let me take care of you." Not that I knew what I was doing at all, this was the most intimate I'd been with anyone. Somehow though, I felt confident in my skills as a lover.

Derrick sat up and said, "This is your first time. I want this to be an experience you'll never forget. Let me make you feel good. You can take care of me next time." *Who could argue with that reasoning?* His lips pressed against mine briefly before he moved back down the bed. Fisting the sheets, I moaned as his tongue flicked against my clit. Nothing would ever cause me to forget such pleasure. I ran my fingers through his hair as quivers of ecstasy coursed through my body. My eyes rolled back in my head, and I bit my lip as an enormous grin filled my face. *Wow.*

He stood up to remove his boxer briefs, and I shivered with anticipation as he slipped on a condom. He positioned himself over me once more. "You're sure this is what you want?" I nodded my affirmation silently. With a hot, breathy whisper against my ear, he said, "Let me know if I need to stop." His tongue flicked out to lick my sensitive earlobe, and then his teeth gently bit down on it as he pressed himself inside me. I cried out as my body was rocked with intense pleasure and only a moment of pain.

He paused to look at me for reassurance, and I pressed my hands against his muscular chest, growling seductively. "Please, I want you, Derrick. Don't stop."

For the next few hours, we explored each other's bodies repeatedly. We took turns pleasing one another, both climaxing several times. My inexperience didn't seem to be noticeable. There was no fumbling or awkward moments, only moments of pure bliss. At last, we collapsed on the bed, out of breath and spent.

Derrick was an attentive lover before, during, and after. He draped the sheet across my body, then kissed me chastely. "I love you, Mary Jane." My stomach let out a long, fierce growl of hunger before I could return the sentiment.

"Well, that was super sexy," I said, mortified at the ruined moment.

"You must be starving. How about I order us some room service? Or would you rather go out?"

"Room service. The longer I can keep you naked, the better," I said, suddenly feeling very comfortable.

"You know, I was thinking the same thing. I'm fine if we stay naked all weekend." He grinned against my lips as he kissed me again. Leaning over me, he grabbed the room service menu off the nightstand. From downstairs, we ordered a full meal, appetizer, and dessert. Normally I wouldn't eat so much in front of a guy, but I felt so comfortable with Derrick, it didn't matter.

As soon as he hung up the phone, he rolled back to hover above me. "They said it will be about thirty minutes. What will we do to pass the time?" The grin on his face was sly and full of innuendo.

"Hmm… well, you ordered a lot of food. Maybe we should work up a bigger appetite."

His whispered, "You read my mind," before his lips found mine once more.

We were able to get in two more times before a knock sounded at the door.

The first silver-lidded plate Derrick brought to the bed contained fresh fruit. He lifted a piece of watermelon toward me.

"That's a big piece," I said, leaning away from his hand.

"Trust me, open your mouth." He placed half the piece of watermelon between my lips, leaned forward, then put his lips over the other half. Biting down together, the sweet juices coated our lips as our tongues moved to capture more of the sweetness. "Damn, I'll never get tired of the taste of you."

When the watermelon juice dripped down, Derrick ran his tongue over my chest, catching the juice and making me want to forego eating.

After filling our stomachs and working the food off a couple more times, we fell asleep wrapped in each other's arms. The next morning, I opened my eyes and smiled as I felt Derrick's body pressed up against mine with his arm across my stomach. Today was the first time I'd awakened in bed with a man. I could get used to this real fast.

"Good morning, beautiful," he whispered a moment before his lips grazed my neck. When I rolled over to face him, he smiled brightly. "Damn, woman, you're stunning even first thing in the morning."

There was no way to respond without sounding cheesy or stumbling on my words, so I pressed my lips to his instead. Derrick slipped on a condom just before I tossed my leg across his waist and lowered myself onto him. As he slid inside me with ease, I gasped and sat back, the sheet falling from my body, exposing me to him. His large hands cupped my breasts as I moved above him, and I placed my hand over his to press harder. He relaxed his head back on the pillow, closed his eyes, and sighed with contentment.

Afterward, I moved back on my side of the bed. He leaned over and pressed light kisses along my cheek. "How do you feel?"

"Amazing." Even that word was not enough to accurately describe everything I felt.

"So, I made your first time memorable?" he asked.

"I'll never forget this, Derrick." My body certainly wouldn't forget the pleasure; my mind wouldn't forget the way he looked, and more than anything, my heart would never forget how gentle he was with me.

For two days, we rarely left the bedroom. Our plans to sightsee dissipated in favor of spending all our time together without any interruptions. We didn't spend the entire time having sex, but we didn't bother with clothes much. For most of the time, we talked about our favorite things.

At one point, Derrick told me about Katelyn's infant years and his struggle with being a single dad. In between our talks, he'd take a moment to call and check on Katelyn. Derrick was drop-dead sexy, sweet, funny, and mature, a perfect man any woman would want. I loved all those things about him, but the thing I loved most was seeing him with Katelyn. Even the thought of having a child at sixteen terrified me. I'm not sure I could've done as well as a mother as he did as a father. The beautiful thing was he'd never considered her a nuisance or a mistake. Even in the privacy of our room where he could tell me anything, he admitted he never once wished he'd given her up.

On the last morning of our trip, we awoke in each other's arms as usual. "This has been the best weekend of my life." Derrick planted kisses on my skin after each word he spoke. "I need a shower, care to join me?"

"Tempting as it is, I think I'll order us breakfast. After your shower, I want to talk to you about something." Our weekend together was special, and I put off the serious conversation as long as possible in case it caused a disagreement between us. I didn't want anything to ruin the memory of our first time together.

Derrick's forehead creased with worry. "Nothing serious, right?"

"Well, it's serious, but not bad." I teased him with my riddles. Nothing about what I needed to say was a bad thing, but I wasn't sure how Derrick would feel about the decision I had to make. Shoving him playfully from the bed, I said, "Go get your shower, stinky."

"Ouch, harsh." He winked as he streaked through the hotel room.

Derrick's phone rang while he was in the shower. It was Gracie's number, so I answered it. "Hey, Gracie!"

"MJ? I wasn't expecting you to answer. Where's Derrick?" After the past year, the sound of concern in Gracie's voice alarmed me.

"He's in the shower. What's wrong?"

"Katelyn's sick. She's running a fever, and we're at the

hospital having her checked out right now. Luckily, these Collins' boys are prepared, and he has Ashton listed as a guardian who can approve healthcare services. I need to let Derrick know though. He thought it was a small cold when he left. He said she got it every time the weather changed because of—"

"Because of her asthma? He told me. What's different this time? Is it serious?" I stepped toward the bathroom door, listening to see if the shower was still running.

"She woke up this morning with a fever, and the doctor said, based on her symptoms, it could be the flu." Each word came out quicker than the last, a sign Gracie was beginning to panic.

"Hang on, Gracie." I knocked on the bathroom door. "Derrick?"

Opening the door, Derrick tugged me inside, pressing his lips to mine before I could speak. "Couldn't wait another second for me, could you?" he teased as his mouth moved to my neck.

Pushing him away gently, I leaned back and held the phone out to him. "It's Gracie."

Instantly, he took the phone and panicked. "Is it Katelyn? What's wrong?" He nodded as Gracie relayed the same information to him. "I can't believe I haven't called you guys today. I got distracted. I'm usually on top of these things."

Distracted? I distracted him from thinking of his daughter and pulled him over two hundred miles away from her when she needed him. His momentary neglect was my fault. If anything happened to her, if I'd kept him from being by her side, I'd never forgive myself. Katelyn was the most important person in Derrick's life, and she always should come first.

Even though it had been my first time and not Derrick's, we still both shared an amazing moment in our lives together. I thought that, if I broke things off and told him what I needed to tell him, he'd think I used him. I never wanted to tarnish our last few days together with a misunderstanding in the way. The news I had would have to wait; it would be better not to tell him. He had more important things to worry about right then. As soon as Katelyn was better, we could talk things over more.

While Derrick finished his phone call, I packed his bag and placed it by the door. After saying goodbye, he rushed into the bedroom. "I need to pa—" He stopped when he saw his bag sitting by the door. "Oh."

"You need to go. I'll check us out of here and take care of everything. Your daughter needs you." To say I wasn't disappointed to end our weekend would be a lie. We would lose a few hours together, but Katelyn's health was most important.

Embracing me, he leaned his forehead against mine. "I love you, MJ. Thank you for understanding. You're amazing, you know that?" I smiled, and Derrick grabbed his backpack and threw it over his shoulder. "I'll call you when I get home and let you know how Katelyn is. I know you are worried too." A quick kiss on the lips, and he disappeared into the hallway.

Being in the hotel room by myself only made me miss Derrick more. I decided to check out early myself. For six hours, I tried to think of anything but the last few days. After getting gas, I plugged my iPod in to listen to an audiobook. The idea was to drift away into the mind of my favorite author, but instead, I worried about Katelyn.

Derrick should've been home taking care of her instead of having sex with me in a hotel. This scenario was one that kept me from wanting a long-distance relationship in the first place. Not that Gracie and Ashton were to blame for Katelyn getting sick, but if Derrick had been there, he would have known how bad it was sooner.

Halfway home, I received a text.

Derrick: I made it home safe, and I'm with Katie. I'll keep you posted. Love you.

Katelyn stayed overnight in the hospital until her fever broke and they could get her hydrated. For the next week, Derrick kept her home from school until she was better. Each night I called to check on her, Derrick and I would talk for hours while he sat by her bedside. And after every conversation, the guilt worsened.

On the day before she returned to school, he called to let me speak to her, and I finally felt relief because she sounded like her old self again.

Not much had changed, but we missed each other. Being intimate had made the distance feel longer. Derrick brought up the Atlanta trip and wanted to make plans for another. No matter what excuse I made, he had a solution. If I couldn't take time off work, he'd make the full trip down. He researched flights and knew he could get a decent deal and have more time with me over a weekend.

March was a peak time in the parks due to spring break, which meant I wouldn't get time off. When I told him I wouldn't be able to hang out much, he offered to buy tickets to get in the park so we could have lunch together and he could be there when I got off work. In the end, I asked him to give me a few days to figure something out. Cameron called me up one night, and in the middle of the conversation, he asked me about Derrick.

"You still have a year and five months of your internship left. Are you going to avoid seeing Derrick to protect his daughter?" On Facetime, he couldn't hide his annoyance with my indecision.

"Cameron, the guilt is eating me up. Katelyn needs Derrick more than I do." In my best dramatic impression, I said, "If it's meant to be, we'll find our way back to one another."

"Life isn't always like the movies, MJ."

"I know. It's one of the reasons I can't make this work. Real life doesn't always get the happy ending." As hard as it was, I had to sacrifice my happiness for Katelyn's. She was at an age where her father was her life. I didn't want to be the person to come between them.

With a trembling hand, I dialed Derrick's number. It took me four tries to hit the correct name in my contacts list. When it finally went through, Derrick answered on the second ring. "Hey, baby. I was just thinking about you."

"Hi, Derrick…" The emotions I'd been holding in spilled out in my voice.

"What's wrong, MJ? Are you crying, sweetheart?"

"Do you have time to talk?" I managed to ask.

"I always have time for you. What's wrong? Hold on a second." Derrick set the phone down for a moment. "Sweetie, MJ's upset right now and needs to talk to Daddy about grown-up stuff. I'll let you talk to her another time, okay?"

In the distance, I heard Katelyn's small voice reply, "Maybe I can cheer her up. Please let me say hi, Daddy."

I knew talking to Katelyn could potentially break me in two. Even hearing her voice made me question my decision again.

Picking up the phone once more, Derrick asked, "Do you mind if Katelyn says hello?"

"Of course not," I lied, my heart aching.

"Hi, MJ. Daddy said you were sad right now. I wanted to come on here and tell you I'm going to draw you a picture and have Daddy text it to you. Is that okay?" How could I tell her no? Once this call ended, I knew I'd probably never see her picture, but I couldn't turn her down.

"That would be wonderful, Katie-cat."

"I love you, MJ." Open wound, pour in salt, repeat. Nothing could match the pain inside from hearing her say those words. Katelyn could be my daughter for the amount of love I had for her. "Does that make you smile?"

As the tears fell, a smile spread across my face, a look

that would have been heartbreaking to a small girl. "Yes, baby girl, that makes me smile so much. I love you too, never forget that."

Derrick came back on the line and said, "She's a great girl, isn't she?"

"Definitely. She takes after her daddy for sure," I said.

"Yep, you know what else we have in common. I love you, only it's probably a lot more than she does." He whispered the last part so Katelyn didn't take offense. Doing this over the phone proved too much to handle. "You're quiet, sweetheart. Did I say something wrong?"

"Nope. You never do. I'm sorry, Derrick."

"Sorry for what?"

"The reason I'm calling… I think you know as well as I do, this isn't working as we hoped it would." He answered with silence. "The long-distance thing, it's too difficult. I can't ask you to give up time with Katelyn to come see me. When my internship is over, we can explore this again if there's still a chance for us." More silence. With a quick glance at the phone, I knew he hadn't hung up. "Derrick, say something, please." Still there was nothing.

After a moment, I heard a sniffle, and I choked back more tears knowing he was crying on the other end of the line. Nothing made me cry more than seeing or hearing a man cry. Men were supposed to be so strong, so when one cried, it seemed much more devastating.

"Daddy?" I heard Katelyn's voice call out. "Are you sad now too?"

I heard Derrick's hand slide across the speaker as he

tried to muffle the sound. It was barely audible, but I heard him say, "Yeah, Daddy's pretty sad, sweetheart." Grunting as something fell on him, he dropped the phone, and I heard, "Hugs from you always make it better." His voice was still laced with sadness, and I knew, even at her young age, Katelyn didn't believe him for a minute.

A few moments later, he replied, "I'm here, MJ." He sighed. "I want to fight you on this. I want to fight for us. The thing is, I know you, and you're stubborn. So this is my proposition to you. Take a while to think this through. I'm not going anywhere, and I don't want anyone else." My heart told me to be selfish and beg him to wait for me, to save himself for my return. Then my pesky brain had to remind me I couldn't keep him from living his life.

"I can't ask you to wait on me, Derrick. Believe me, I wanted this to work more than anyone. You need to be with Katie though. And while we're apart, if you meet the girl of your dreams, you should be able to pursue her."

"I already did. She's on the phone with me right now." Derrick sighed again. "Cheesy but true. Lines aside, I love you, Mary Jane. The best things in life are worth waiting for, and you're worth it."

"I love you too, and Katelyn. That's why I need to do this. Promise me one thing and mean it. If you meet a woman who sparks your interest, don't hesitate. Ask her out and make sure you're not giving up your happily ever after on me." After a long pause of thought, he agreed to my terms.

After that phone call, we went our separate ways for the most part. At first, Derrick called once a week, and then it fell to every couple of weeks. After a while, we kept in touch mostly through Gracie.

Chapter Ten

DERRICK

The day was perfect for fishing with the sun shining, warm temperatures, and a nice, cool breeze. Sitting on the dock, I cast my line out first. Ashton took a seat next to me and cast his out next. Fishing with him was something we did as kids with our father running the show. Having Katelyn in my life, I didn't get to go much anymore. Gracie was kind enough to take care of Katelyn so we could enjoy some brother time.

Taking a deep breath of fresh air, Ashton released a sigh of delight. "Last time I was here was with Gracie. It was about this time of year." His face screwed up in thought before he corrected himself. "It was November actually, so we're about a month early. You know she fell in, and her catch tugged my fishing pole under water?"

I listened to him, but every time I heard Gracie's name, I thought of Mary Jane and I couldn't concentrate. My lack of interest in his story went unnoticed.

"In a few years, I want to bring Autumn and teach her how to fish. You should bring Katie sometime. She's at the right age."

I nodded, still staring ahead at the water, battling the thoughts in my head.

"Gracie is going down to Florida in a few days. You should think about going with her. Spend some time with MJ. I know you miss her."

If I'd been a smart man, I'd have jumped at the chance and called Gracie to make arrangements on the spot. Instead, my idiot personality had taken over to act nonchalant or like a giant asshole.

"Nah. That's in the past. I've moved on," I lied, hoping to avoid having to talk about something still painful for me.

"Come on, man, when I said her name, I saw the look on your face." Ashton pushed further.

"I said I'm over it, so drop it. Please." Seven months had gone by since the last time I talked to Mary Jane. We'd been broken up for eight. Prince Charming wasn't going to lecture me on true love because he had his happy ending. It was easy for someone with a perfect love life to think positively about relationships. When you didn't have anyone though, it was hard to remember anything but the bad stuff.

Ashton and Gracie had a rocky start to their relationship; I hadn't forgotten. Then they were like Prince Charming and Cinderella or something equally mushy and girly. If you were miserable and wanted company, they weren't the ones to be around. Some of us weren't lucky enough to experience such bliss. Not wanting to fight with him over this, I changed the subject instead. "I'd like to bring Katie out. She loves the lake, and I think she'd get a kick out of it. Maybe we can invite Gracie, and the four of us can have a picnic?"

Obviously noticing my avoidance of the touchy subject, Ashton grinned. "Yeah, man, that sounds great. Gracie will love to as long as one of us does all the icky stuff for her." He laughed and clarified. "In her words, she loves the serenity of fishing but not the sliminess. Hence, I have to bait the hook and pull off a fish if she catches one."

"I didn't realize she was so girly," I teased him.

"To hear her tell it, she's not." Ashton laughed.

"Too bad she doesn't have a twin. You lucked out when you found her, man." I meant every word too. I adored my sister-in-law. She was not only gorgeous but one of the strongest people I knew and one of the most loyal friends in the world.

"You'll find your Gracie one day, Derrick. In my opinion though—"

"Don't say it. You can think it all you want, but please don't say it out loud."

Ashton frowned and gave a nod. And that was the last we spoke of it, for a while at least.

***

Getting through another Christmas without Mary Jane beside me was rough, but I focused on Katelyn as always and made it through. When the new year began, I resolved to make things right between us somehow. New Year's Eve I got drunk at Ashton and Gracie's house. Mom and Dad babysat the kids for us so we could ring in the new year with our friends. At midnight, when everyone else had someone to kiss, I texted Mary Jane. The loneliness hit so hard.

Me: Happy New Year, beautiful. I've been a crappy friend, but I promise in the new year to be better.

Mary Jane: Happy New Year to you and Katelyn. Give me a call sometime, friend. :)

A few days later, I picked up the phone to call her when I remembered the text. Before the phone finished dialing, I hung up. Katelyn had been on holiday break, giving me a lot of distractions to keep me busy. When it came time for her to go back to school, I threw myself into work again.

"Katelyn! Get down here! You're going to be late for school!" How did I end up with a five-year-old who took more time to get ready than any grown woman I knew? Then I remembered, her Uncle Cameron.

Cameron taught Katelyn about being fabulous one day, and now her motto was "Always strive to be fabulous." Due to that motto, it took me an hour to get her out of the house each morning.

Katelyn appeared on the stairs wearing black jeans with a white T-shirt. Over the T-shirt, she wore a pink hoodie with sparkles, and on her feet, she had a pair of sparkly pink sandals. At the top of the stairs, she held her arms out. "Do

I look fabulous or what?"

"Completely. Let's go. You have a packed lunch in the kitchen. Go grab it and put it in your backpack. The car is warming, and if we're not on the road in five minutes, you'll be late."

"Chillax, Daddy-O." She held her left hand palm out to me as though telling me to talk to the hand. Mentally adding Cameron to my shit list for turning my child into a drama queen, I took a deep breath.

"Look here, I'm about to ground you from talking to your Uncle Cameron."

Placing her tiny hands over her mouth, she tried to stifle a giggle. Sometimes I thought she only did this stuff to get me riled up. After struggling for several minutes to leave the house, we got to the car, and I made sure she was buckled in safely. A quick kiss and an "I love you, Daddy" gave me back my sweet girl just before she ran off to beat the school bell. Keeping my eye on the Rainbow Dash backpack, I watched to make sure she got inside before driving away.

Just as my fist was about to collide with the door, it swung open. Finger to his lips, Ashton mouthed, "Shh, Autumn's asleep." Ashton was a stay-at-home dad. It was refreshing to see him go through some of the same experiences I did so I had someone with whom I could share stories. Not too many of my friends had kids. "Let's go downstairs. I've got a baby monitor."

"Where's your beautiful wife?" I asked as we settled into

his downstairs rec room. Every time I was in this room, I remembered the way I first met her, Gracie on the pool table in nothing but a button-down shirt. I felt like an asshat that day when I interrupted them.

"She's sleeping. We've been taking turns getting up at night with Autumn. Last night was her night." Placing a roll of blueprints on the table, he unrolled it flat and placed a coffee mug at each corner. "I can't believe we're finally doing this, man."

Blueprints of our club in front of us, it was almost unreal to think we were designing a dream come true after years of only talking about it. A building on Broadway became vacant, and Ashton was able to get it cheap from a friend. For the last few months, we'd been working hard on the plans to get everything designed and ready for business.

"Look here, bitches. I know you're not starting this without me here!" Cameron came barreling down the stairs, making his presence known as usual. He smacked my ass and then Ashton's. "Dammit, you Collins' boys are built so nicely." Gavin cleared his throat as he came in behind him. Cameron wrapped his arm around his husband and kissed his cheek. "You know you're the only one for me."

"Hey, Gavin, do me a favor and tell your husband to stop teaching my daughter his diva ways." Gavin and Ashton snickered at my annoyance.

Cameron looked offended as he shouted, "Stop that nonsense talk! There's nothing wrong with fabulousness."

"You may get your wish, Derrick. We found out today our surrogate is having a girl. Cameron will have someone else to teach all his fabulous ways." Cameron and Gavin were having a baby via surrogate, and she was due in five months. Best friends, married to brothers, now Cameron and Gracie would even have babies only a few months apart. Being whipped by our daughters, Ashton and I knew they were in for an amazing adventure.

Silent cheers and manly one-arm hugs were exchanged. "Do we ever get to meet this surrogate?" I asked. As far as I knew, no one had ever met the girl.

"She prefers to stay anonymous. She was already so generous to do this for us with nothing in return but the cost of her medical expenses. I'll tell you though, she's gorgeous. With her genes and Cameron's mixed together, we're going to have a beautiful baby." As he spoke of his unborn child, Gavin's eyes sparkled and his smile brightened the room.

Justin Bieber's "Baby" screamed from Cameron's phone. "What's up, gorgeous?" After a brief pause, he peered up at me and turned to walk upstairs.

"Where are you going, Cam? We've got blueprints and décor to design," I shouted after him.

And a moment later, I felt Ashton's fist connect with my bicep. "Shh!" As the upstairs door opened, Autumn's cries could be heard. "Crap. I'll be back. I'm going to bring Autumn down here so Gracie can sleep."

I followed Ashton upstairs so I could fix drinks for everyone and saw Cameron with Autumn in his arms softly singing to her.

"What happened to your phone call?" I asked, watching him calm the baby as if he did this every day.

"I told her I'd call her back. I love spending time with this little one." Peering down at the now content pink bundle in his arms, Cameron's grin widened.

"You're pretty great with her, Cam," I said genuinely.

"Thanks. It's a little frightening. I don't know how you did this alone, man."

"I won't lie. It's not a piece of cake." Being a teenager with a baby was tough, even with two grandparents willing to help. Though they were around a lot, I raised Katelyn for the most part on my own. There were many nights I spent pacing the floor with her only to turn around and have to attend school to finish out my senior year to graduate. Having a baby at such a young age caused me to mature quicker than most men.

Gracie stumbled out of the bedroom with her hair sticking up in several different directions. Wearing baggy flannel pajama pants with a tank top splotched in baby spit, she grunted in annoyance. Cameron turned and handed me the baby without pause. "Good golly, Miss Molly, what the hell happened to you?" With each word, the pitch in his voice went higher.

"This is what motherhood looks like," Gracie said as she yawned and rubbed her hands over her mouth to remove the dried spittle.

"That's what motherhood looks like on Damien's mother. Did you fucking roll in the dirt and stick your finger in a wall socket?"

Gracie rolled her eyes, flipped Cameron off, and stumbled into the kitchen.

She poured a cup of coffee and brought it up to her nose, inhaling the intoxicating aroma, causing a smile of bliss to appear on her face before taking a small sip. "What are my guys up to this morning?"

"We were about to go over the plans for Club Cameron. I need a break so I can save you from yourself. Let's go get you naked," Cameron said, grasping her arm and trying to lead her away.

Ashton walked in at that moment. "Normally I wouldn't be too happy to hear another man ask my wife to get naked. In this case, Cameron, please pamper her. She deserves it."

"Are you agreeing I'm hideous?" Gracie asked, sounding a bit hurt. Hormones messed with a woman during and after pregnancy. Come to think of it, hormones messed a woman up at any time, but I was too smart a guy to say it out loud.

"Bug, you couldn't look hideous if you tried. I want him to pamper you so you can relax and feel better." Gracie's face softened into a loving smile as Ashton leaned forward and kissed her. Ashton was lucky to have had two great loves in his life, and I envied him for it. They say nice guys finish last; for Ashton, it wasn't true in the least. Between the two of us, I was the bad boy, and I seemed to be the one who always finished last. In high school, I had several girlfriends before I got one of them pregnant. Being a single dad was attractive to women, but not when I was a teenager.

As much as I avoided talking about her with others, Mary Jane never drifted far from my thoughts. The only way to keep from breaking down was not to talk about it. I'd dialed her number at least a hundred times in the last nine months. A month after breaking up, we stopped talking on the phone. She sent me an occasional text checking in, but I always gave short answers. With the exception of my drunk text, I mostly texted her pictures of Katelyn.

Cameron latched his hand over Gracie's arm and turned back to us. "You boys go downstairs and start without me on the dull stuff. When I finish with my Gracie girl here, I'll be down to make your lives more exciting with my presence."

Ashton, Gavin, and I went back downstairs to return to work. After an hour, we took a break to wait on Cameron, who hadn't shown his face again. Pouring each of us a steamy, fresh cup of coffee, Gavin handed a mug to me before the questions began again. "Have you heard from MJ?" His eyebrows rose above the glass as he took a drink.

"Not since New Year's Eve. I promised to be a better friend this year, but I haven't been keeping the promise so far. I was thinking about going down to see her, with Katelyn, as a surprise."

Ashton cleared his throat nervously. "I'm not sure that's a good idea."

"You're the one always trying to convince me not to give up on her. Is there something you know that I don't? Is she seeing someone?" It hadn't occurred to me she could have met someone. I didn't know why. She was in a new place and could've met someone quickly enough. Any guy would be lucky to be with a sexy, vivacious woman such as her.

Ashton cleared his throat and said, "No, nothing like that. With what you told me about how she ended things, I think it'd be better to wait for her to come back to you when her internship is over. You two tried the long-distance thing, and it didn't go the way you hoped. Be patient with her. It wouldn't hurt to answer her call though, but face to face wouldn't be good for either of you."

"It's difficult, Ash. Not being with her is driving me crazy," I said, not considering who I was talking to.

"At least she isn't dating an abusive asshole you can't save her from. That is something hard to get over. I still kick myself for not seeing how bad he was for her." Ashton never had forgiven himself for what happened to Gracie. Instead, he strived to make every day perfect for her.

"Sorry, man. That was stupid of me to say." Before he responded, Ashton's eyes widened, and a smile graced his lips as he glanced at something over my shoulder. I turned to see Gracie come in the room. "Wow, you look like a different woman."

She smiled. "Normally I'd flip you off for the backhanded compliment, but I appreciate it right now. So, are you calling it Club Cameron?"

After Ashton and I had a nice long belly laugh, he responded, "He's dreaming. We haven't decided on a name yet."

Ashton and Gracie shared an intimate moment as he went to dote on her. I turned my attention to the blueprints again, trying to drown out the noise of their kisses behind me.

"We're being rude to Derrick," Gracie said as she moved out of Ashton's arms to occupy the space next to me. She placed her hand on my shoulder as she leaned over to glance at the designs. "This looks amazing!"

"Thanks," I responded.

"You guys, this place is going to be a hit, and I know it. Now we need to think of a name. Personally, I think Gracie's would be perfect." She winked and then leaned up on her tiptoes to kiss my cheek.

"It's no wonder you and Cam are so close," I teased. "We've been throwing around a few names. Nothing seems perfect yet."

"I'm going to run upstairs to check on Autumn," Ash called from behind us.

Gracie took the opportunity to pull me over to the couch. "Sit down. We need to talk." It was obvious this would be a talk about Mary Jane. She was the topic of every conversation we'd ever had. "Ashton's birthday is coming up, and I want to do something special for him. I thought we could get the whole family together and go to dinner at his favorite restaurant." It must've been evident on my face I hadn't expected Ashton to be the topic. "What's wrong?"

"Nothing, I was expecting a different talk."

She nodded and then placed her hand on my leg. "You thought I was going to ask you about MJ?" It was more of a rhetorical question because she didn't wait for an answer. "She misses you. I know because we talk almost every day. And you and Katelyn make up most of our conversations. Her internship is over in seven months, and she may move back home. If she does…"

"If she does, we'll cross that bridge when we get to it." I lifted the coffee mug from the table and brought it to my nose to breathe in the strong aroma of the French roast.

Gracie gasped. "I got it! A Shot in the Dark."

"What is?" I asked as I scrambled to keep my cup from spilling over when I was startled by her excitement.

"The club name, A Shot in the Dark." Energy radiated from her as she shared her train of thought. "Clubs are dark, you'll serve shots… It's a pun. Plus, a shot in the dark means a hopeful attempt, which is what you're doing by opening this club."

"I like it! We could even have a menu specifically for individual shots. We could have a game where you're blindfolded and must name the shots for free drinks or a name on the wall, something gimmicky along those lines," I exclaimed. "It's perfect. When Ash gets back down here, we'll run it by him, but I think you just named our club."

Seeming pleased with herself, Gracie ran up the stairs, yelling behind her, "I'll be back in a minute."

A moment after she disappeared, her phone rang. Mary Jane's name popped up, and I let it go to voice mail until she called back again twice. The third time I answered, assuming it was an emergency. "Gracie!" she called out as soon as I answered it. Taking Ashton's advice, I grinned at the happiness in her voice and was about to speak when she started giggling. "Tristan, stop!" Two simple words felt like a punch in the gut. "Hello?" she said when she heard nothing from my end.

Gracie appeared in front of me. I held the phone out to her and said, "It's MJ. She called three times, so I thought it was an emergency. From the sounds of it, I was wrong."

She'd told me about her friendship with Tristan, but the way she said his name right then didn't sound friendly; it sounded flirtatious, and it awoke the green-eyed monster of jealousy inside me.

Gracie took the phone from me and said, "Hello? MJ? Yeah, it's me. No, it was a friend of mine who answered my phone for me." She mouthed "I'm sorry" to me, and I waved my hand, letting her know not to worry. "Oh… um… yeah, let me call you back in just a minute."

She hung up the phone and said, "Tristan is a good friend, that's all."

"No one has to explain anything to me. She's free to be with whoever she wants. Look, I need to go. I have to pick Katelyn up from school. Tell Ash I'll call him later."

On my way to Katelyn's school, I tried desperately to quit hearing Mary Jane's giggles in my head. The line at the school was full of cars with parents anxiously waiting for the school day to end. A woman walked past my car then stopped, ducked down to look in the windshield, and waved. I rolled down the window when she stepped back to stand by the door.

"Hey, Derrick, right? Katie's dad?" She pushed a strand of her dark auburn hair back behind her ear in a nervous fashion and added, "I'm her teacher, Melanie Harris. We met on the first day of school."

"Of course, how are you, Mrs. Harris?"

"It's Ms., and you can call me Lanie." Her lips formed a

soft smile, and then she ran her tongue along them slowly. "Katie's a joy to have in class."

"That's nice to hear. Who's watching the class right now?"

"Oh, they had an assembly this afternoon, so everyone's in the gym. It's my week to direct traffic after school." She leaned forward, placing her elbows on the window frame, which put our faces closer than I was used to for cordial conversation. "Did you travel any over the holidays?"

"Nope, not really."

"Oh, Katelyn's been talking about Disney a lot, so I assumed you'd be going this summer."

"No, probably not. Katelyn and I have a friend who works there that she wants to see, but it's not looking possible this year." The bell rang, alerting the waiting parents the kids would be out in only a few minutes.

Lanie glanced back to check the sidewalk and noticed the kids were trickling out slowly. She returned to face me and asked, "This may seem weird, but would you like to grab a coffee with me sometime?"

I was being hit on by a hot elementary school teacher; that was strange to me. Women flirted with me quite often; I just hadn't paid much attention to it lately. At first I wanted to say no, and then I heard the giggling and the "Tristan, stop" ringing through my head, and I decided there was nothing wrong with saying, "Yes, I'd love to."

Being forward, she reached her hand inside the car. "Give me your phone and I'll put my number in." I watched as her fingers moved lithely over the keyboard while she bit her lip in concentration. "I look forward to hearing from you." She turned to walk away and then twisted around one last time to give me a flirty wave. With a thin white blouse with a silk scarf around her neck, straight black knee-length skirt, and subtle black heels, she was the epitome of the dirty librarian fantasy most guys had. Her curvy hips made a nice shimmy as she walked away. It wasn't the emotional attachment I felt to Mary Jane when I met her, but I was attracted to this woman physically at least.

The moment I got home with Katelyn, I sent her upstairs to do her homework. I'd been terribly lonely lately and was excited to see if I had anything in common with someone new. If Mary Jane was moving on, so was I.

"Lanie? Hi, it's Derrick."

"Hi. I didn't know if you'd call me today or not. I was afraid I might have come on too strongly."

"No, you didn't. I'd love to have coffee with you, but would it be okay? With you being Katelyn's teacher and all, I mean." Even though she was Katelyn's teacher, I wouldn't break my rule of not bringing her around my daughter like I did with Mary Jane.

She laughed nervously. "I think so. I've never done this before, and first grade isn't exactly big in the scandalous grades. I don't think anyone will accuse me of playing favorites. I've wanted to get to know you since I first met you."

"That's very flattering for a guy to hear from a beautiful woman like you. Are you free on Saturday?"

There wasn't even a pause as she answered, "Yes." As

plans came together for a date, my guilt began to set in. It was silly of me to feel guilty when Mary Jane and I weren't together anymore, but somehow it still felt as though I was cheating on her, and I hated the feeling.

As I sat there pondering the guilt, I decided to do something about it. The moment her voice came on the line, I regretted making the call. "Hi, MJ. It's Derrick. Are you busy?"

"Derrick? Wow, it's been a long time. I'm getting ready for work, but I have a few minutes. Is something wrong?"

"I've been ignoring your calls lately, and I hate myself for it. It's not how a friend should act. I wanted to explain myself."

Before I could explain anything, she spoke up. "You have nothing to apologize for. It's been hard for me too, not hearing your voice or talking to you. I miss you more than I can say, Derrick."

"I miss you too."

"In about six months, I'll be coming back to Nashville."

"In July, not September?" Since she left in September, I assumed she'd return in the same month after two years.

"It's like a school semester for the program. It will end early June, and I'll be home by July." Suddenly the time frame seemed so short, and I regretted making the date.

"It's sort of the reason I called. I asked someone out today. It may not go anywhere, but I wanted you to know." Not only did I want to take back the words, but I dreaded the date now.

Silence filled the connection, and I had to make sure

we were still on the phone. After a moment, Mary Jane said, "It's getting a little late. I need to get to work. Take care, Derrick, and tell Katie-cat hello for me, if it's not too awkward."

"She'd love to know you're thinking about her. Can I call you again sometime?" Hearing her voice today had stirred something inside of me. It made me want more.

"Please do. I'll talk to you soon." After a short pause, she added, "And good luck with your date." The hurt in her voice had been apparent, but not my intention. I wanted a redo. Telling her about the date had been my way of judging if her feelings for me had changed. It was obvious to me now they hadn't.

Chapter Eleven

MARY JANE

"Hola, Chica!" followed by the sound of keys clanking against the kitchen table alerted me to Angel being home. Most days I felt fine and went on with life as normal. Other days, I curled up in bed to listen to depressing music while propping my feet up to keep them from swelling more. Angel sauntered in, noticed my sad expression and asked, "Chica, what's wrong? Move over, girl." I slid over, making room for her to curl up next to me.

"I miss Derrick. I heard a song earlier by the band Halestorm. Remember, you, Gracie, and me saw them perform in Nashville a few years ago? It was called 'Break In,' and it stirred up my hormones something fierce."

"Have you talked to him?" Her fingers trailed through my stringy blonde hair, smoothing it away from my face.

"He called me a little more than a month ago, and we talked briefly. It was still pretty hard for both of us." Talking about Derrick having a date wasn't something I could handle, so I conveniently left that part of the conversation out. Changing the subject, I asked, "Are we going to move back to Nashville or stay here?"

Angel pondered briefly before saying, "I'd like to go home, back to Nashville. I miss the gang, especially our Gracie. Can you handle going back there and seeing Derrick if things don't work out between you?"

"I'm pretty sure the Derrick ship sailed or sank long ago. I screwed up my chance with him by pushing him away. I'm with you. Nashville is home. I didn't want to leave you or make you move though if it wasn't what you wanted."

Angel moved with me so I wouldn't be alone. If she wanted to stay now, I had to give her a chance to let me repay the favor. "We have about four months, so when do we start looking for a place to live?"

"No time better than now. Let's see what we can find." Grabbing my laptop off the nightstand, we began searching for housing back home.

The prospect of moving back heightened my mood, until I got to work the next day. On a break, I was researching housing for us on my tablet when Tristan sat down. "Hello, beautiful, whatcha doing?"

My eyes remained focused on the computer screen as I said nonchalantly, "Trying to find a house for Angel and me in Nashville."

A clanging noise caused me to glance up. Tristan's fork had fallen to the table, his mouth gaped open, and his eyes bulged in shock. "What? Why? When?"

"House. My internship's up. Four months." I answered the questions in the order he asked them.

"MJ, you're my best friend. You can't leave me." His eyes became a little misty with tears, and it broke my heart. Tristan had been one of my closest friends since I moved here. We'd spent every day together. We even scheduled our days off the same in order to do things together. I hadn't realized how hard it would be to lose him until now.

"T, you know you're my best friend. Nashville is my home though. My family is there, blood and chosen. You could come with us. Move to Nashville, start over like you've always wanted. Bring your little sister. Maybe she'll do better there."

"You don't think she'd be bullied in Nashville too?" he asked skeptically.

"You never know. A new start, new town, a new chance to make friends, it may be exactly what she needs. I know of a public high school there, specifically for exceptional children. She could fit in. I can get information for you to see if she can attend." He was considering it. I could almost see the wheels of thought turning in his head. If Tristan moved with us, then I knew I could get through this move back with or without Derrick waiting for me. "Well?"

"Let me think about it. I'll let you know." Tristan stood up, tossed his uneaten lunch in the trash, and walked out the door.

March was part of peak season at the park, which meant the crowds were so thick people were shoulder to shoulder. As I shoved my way through the hordes of people, I kept an eye out for Tristan, though I'd never find him in the crowd. We had a tradition of meeting at the parking lot after work each day in order to plan our evening entertainment. When I got to our regular bench, a teenage couple was locked in a serious make-out session.

In the last year, we'd been close, so I'd learned that sometimes he just needed room to breathe. I sent him a text to give him an out.

Me: Headed home for the night. I have a headache. Love you, T.

I love you had become a normal thing for us, but there had never been anything intimate between us, only a purely friendly love.

When I got home, I went straight to my bed and popped in a movie to pass the time. My phone was strategically placed directly in my peripheral vision so I'd know immediately if Tristan responded. My mind wasn't focusing on the movie; instead, I drifted into a memory of a day I spent with Tristan last year.

It was during the off-season at the parks, which meant the rides for lines were almost nonexistent, except on weekends of course. We chose a warm sunny day in February to have Tristan help his sister Macy have a day of fun away from school. When I first laid eyes on her, I wanted to cry. He knocked on the door, and as I opened it, she was standing there with her arms wrapped around his waist. Her hair was slowly growing back though it still had the appearance of a buzz cut. She had a ribbon tied around her head to offer a sense of femininity.

"Hi, Macy, I'm Mary Jane. You can call me MJ."

She smiled shyly, then softly responded, "Hi, MJ."

"Tristan, if you'll wait for us in here, I have a surprise for Macy."

When I found out we'd be spending the day together, I went to the costume department for help. A girl named Summer helped me to find the perfect accessory, colorful streaked wigs, so we could both wear one and no one would think anything of it other than we were having fun. "Do you prefer purple or pink?"

"Pink," she said with a smile, wondering what was coming. I lifted her wig out of the bag. It was light pink with soft curls and stripes of dark blue. My wig was purple with pale pink streaks throughout. She clapped in excitement and said, "I love it!"

"Grab whatever accessories you want to wear. Earrings, scarves, shoes if they're not too big. Have at it."

When she finished shopping through the closet, she came out with a new attitude on life. She was smiling and twirling around to show me her ensemble.

"You look great! Now help me?" I let her choose my outfit for the day. She apparently wanted to match, which was fine with me. I had a purple Tinkerbell tank top I paired

with a set of pale pink capri pants to match my hair.

Tristan waited patiently for us in the living room. When he spotted us, his face lit up. "You guys look awesome!" Macy ran to him, hugging him tightly. He bent to embrace her, then glanced up at me mouthing, "Thank you" with tears misting his eyes.

Kids were coming up to Macy all day, telling her how cool her hair looked, wanting to know where she got her shirt, even guys were smiling and paying attention. At a snack stop in the afternoon, we grabbed ice cream cones to celebrate our fun day. Macy excused herself to go to the restroom, giving Tristan and me a moment alone.

He placed his hand against mine, catching me off guard for a moment. "You are the best friend I could've asked for here. Today has meant the world to Macy, but it's meant even more to me seeing her have fun and be happy." Sliding off his stool, he wrapped his arms around me in a hug. "I love you, MJ."

"Aww, I love you too, T," I responded. From that moment on, we were inseparable as friends and coworkers.

When my mind drifted back to the present, my movie had ended and I'd been staring at the menu screen. Reluctantly, I slid out of bed, trudged over to the DVD player, and put another video in. Curling up in bed watching movies used to be my favorite thing to do after a long day; now it was lonely. Grabbing my phone, I scrolled through the list of names to see who I could call. My finger stopped on Derrick's name. Our last conversation hadn't gone so well.

Although I'd told him I wanted him to move on, hearing he had a date was like a burning poker to the chest. I knew if I called him, I could casually ask how his date went, but did I want to know? "Oh, what the hell," I mumbled out loud before dialing his number.

"Hello?" a female voice answered.

"Oh, I'm sorry I must have the wrong number," I said, thinking Derrick must have changed his number.

"Are you looking for Derrick? My name's Lanie, and he left his phone on the table while he's stepped away to the restroom. Is this Katelyn's babysitter? If you hold on a moment, he'll be right back."

"No, I'm not a babysitter. I'm a… friend."

"Well, would you like me to have him call you back tomorrow? We might be out a bit late tonight," she said with an almost nervous-sounding laugh.

"Um… yeah, I mean, no. You can tell him I called to check on Katie. Thanks." How worse could my timing be than to call him in the middle of his date? The woman hinted as though they would sleep together that night. How long had they been dating? It'd been over a month since we'd spoken; it only took two months for our relationship to grow serious. Standing up, I shook my head free of the thoughts of betrayal. He was out with this woman because I pushed him away. Did I expect him to wait two years for me?

I felt the moisture on my cheeks before I even realized I was crying. My chest felt like someone dropped a boulder on it, and I couldn't breathe. This must be what a broken heart felt like.

The doorbell interrupted my moment of self-pity. Trudging down the hallway, I peeked into Angel's room. The bed was made up and hadn't been slept in again. I knew because I was the one who made her bed. Angel was a slob.

Shoulders slumped, hair disheveled, I opened the door to see Tristan standing there smiling. His smile faded into a worrisome look. "What's wrong?"

Stepping inside he embraced me. I slid my arms under his and brought my hands up to rest on his shoulder blades. His hug caused gasping sobs to explode from me as though I'd lost all control of my emotions. Tristan gently guided me to the couch, then took a seat next to me. He reached across my body to grab a tissue from the table next to me.

"Talk to me, MJ."

"You didn't meet me after work today. What happened?" I said through gasping breaths as I tried to calm myself.

"I needed some time to think. Is that why you're crying?" His look of worry became a look of shame he must have felt at causing me pain.

I shook my head to ease his worries. "No, sweetie." I told him about my phone call to Derrick and the mysterious woman who answered.

"Maybe she's Katelyn's babysitter or possibly a client he's meeting with? Doesn't he run a security company?"

"She asked if I was a babysitter, so that's not it. We spoke recently. He told me then he'd asked someone out. Could my timing have been any more perfect than to call him during their first date? If it's their first date. Forget it, it doesn't matter."

Tristan pushed my hair behind my ear and said, "Of course it matters. You wouldn't be so hurt right now if it didn't. How about I make us some fruit smoothies, and we put in a good horror movie to take our mind off things?"

"Sounds good. Make mine a strawberry banana?" I asked with a forced grin.

"You got it. Why don't you go wash your face and pick out the movie?"

While Tristan went to the kitchen, I slipped into the bathroom to splash water on my face. As I glanced in the mirror, I cringed at how puffy my face looked. Cameron called what I had been doing 'the ugly cry,' and boy there wasn't a more accurate description.

Cabin in the Woods was the movie I picked out for our viewing. Whenever one of us felt lonely or down, we chose a horror movie because no one truly got a happy ending in those, and they wouldn't make us feel worse.

After getting comfortable, I pushed mute on the TV as the menu screen looped. "Did you make a decision about moving?"

Before he could give me a response, my phone rang. Spotting the name, I cringed as I felt emotions building up again. "It's Gracie. I don't think I can talk to her right now."

"Hello?" Tristan answered the phone for me instead. "Um, yeah, Gracie, she's here, but she isn't up to talking. Can I have her call you later?" Tristan listened for a moment, then closed his eyes, pressed his index finger and thumb against the bridge of his nose, and replied, "I'm so sorry. I can tell her or I can let you. Sure, sweetie. I'll tell her, and we'll call you back."

"What's wrong? Is it Ashton? Autumn?" I immediately jumped to panic mode, wondering what made Tristan appear so serious after such a short conversation.

Grabbing my shoulders, he focused my attention on him. "No, MJ, calm down. It's Ashton's father. He was killed in a car accident tonight."

Ashton's father meant Derrick's father, and I made the connection immediately. Knowing how close they were to their father, my heart broke imagining their immense grief.

"Gracie said Ashton called her from Derrick's house a moment ago. Apparently he gave Derrick the news, and he didn't react at all. She said Derrick's in complete disbelief. She wanted you to call him." Tristan paused, probably gauging my reaction to see if I would lose control.

Wiping my eyes, I stood up, straightened my clothes, and marched off to the bedroom yelling behind me, "I'll do better than that." Tristan followed me into the bedroom where I'd already begun packing my bags. While I packed, he called to check flights, which proved futile when he spoke to my doctor who said I couldn't fly in my condition. Without hesitation, he offered to drive me instead.

My manager was very generous in letting me take time off so I could have a chance to attend the funeral and find a place to live as well. Earlier this month, they had offered me a full-time position, but I hadn't told anyone yet. After asking for the time off, I asked for an extension on the decision to stay as well. My mind wasn't in the right place to make any life decisions. Seeing Derrick could change everything about my future, in one way or another.

Tristan asked for the same time off, stating he was also a friend of Derrick's so he could share the ten-hour driving time with me. I texted Gracie to tell her I was on the way, and she offered to let us stay with them. In less than a day, I'd come face to face with Derrick again.

Chapter Twelve

DERRICK

Denial, that was what I felt. My father wasn't dead. My mother wasn't a widow. My daughter would have her grandfather to teach her to drive the way he taught me. Denial, that's what it boiled down to. Ashton didn't want to let me live in denial. Call after call with questions about funeral arrangements, he attempted to help me face reality. After the last time I told him I didn't know, he sighed and hung up.

My brother rarely got angry with anyone, even when they deserved it. And I deserved his anger more than anyone. I'd left him to shoulder the weight of everything, even our mother crying in his arms, as he made the arrangements to spare her that painful act. Since the accident, Gracie hadn't left my mom's side. Saying goodbye and experiencing this loss was impossible for me to do.

My dad has always been my hero. Never once did he turn his back on me, even at sixteen when I told him I knocked up my girlfriend. No anger, no disappointment came from him. He simply said, "We'll get through this, son." When I told him I wanted to raise Katelyn, he said, "I'm proud of you. You'll be an excellent father." Since I learned from the best, I knew he was right.

Ashton received the call about the accident. Knowing Ashton would remain calm in an emergency, Dad had listed him as his emergency contact. I'd barely been home a few minutes from my date with Lanie. He was standing at my door, face scruffy, hair a mess, eyes red from crying; I thought something happened to Gracie or Autumn. Then he placed his hand on my shoulder and said, "Dad was in a car accident. He's gone."

Before I could respond, he jerked me forward against his chest and held onto me as he shook with sobs. Dumbfounded, I patted his back and told him everything was okay. Not believing my own words, I didn't know how they could bring Ashton any comfort. He asked me to go with him to tell mom, but I couldn't. I made up an excuse that I had something to take care of with Katelyn.

Katelyn. I hadn't told her yet. After Ashton had told me, I'd barely slept a wink. The next day I avoided everything, his calls, telling Katelyn, facing reality. A day later, after much thinking, I had no idea how to tell a six-year-old her pawpaw was gone forever. She worshiped the ground he walked on almost as much as he worshipped... had worshipped her.

Everyone would be at Ashton's house tonight for the wake. How was I going to face the overabundance of sympathy thrown at me when I could barely accept a funeral was necessary?

"Daddy?" Katelyn said, rubbing the sleep from her eyes. I'd let her sleep in so I could figure out how to tell her what was going on. I needed her with me today.

"Hey, baby girl. Come here." I held my arms open for her. She embraced me and I hugged her tightly, holding back my emotions. "We need to find you a dress for this evening. We're going to your Uncle Ashton's house."

"Are they having a party?" she asked innocently.

Lifting her up, I stepped back and sat on the edge of the bed with her in my lap. "It's not the type of party you're used to attending. Your pawpaw had an accident in his car."

"Is he okay? Do we need to go see him at the hospital?" Innocent questions bounced from her, making each answer harder to give.

"No, he's not in the hospital. He's in Heaven." My voice cracked on the last sentence, but I kept my emotions in check. "We're going to Uncle Ashton's to celebrate his life and talk about how much we loved him."

"He's in Heaven? Can I still see him once in a while?" Times like these made single parenting the worst. It had to be easier when you could share these burdens with the other parent; at least I hoped it made it half as hard for them.

"You know, let's go find you a dress, and I'll explain this better in a little while." Later I'd have Ashton and Gracie help me through this part.

Katelyn chose a dress her grandparents bought her for Christmas this past year. It was a red sundress with a black velvet ribbon around the waist, not the most appropriate color for a wake, but my dad always loved her in it. Pairing it with a black sweater, I let her wear it for Pawpaw.

Gracie answered the door when we arrived. "Katelyn, you look beautiful, boo." Gracie bent to hug her and then reached for me. She whispered in my ear, "I'm glad you're here." It had occurred to me not to show up, but in the end, I couldn't abandon Ashton.

Gracie took Katelyn's hand and said, "Come with me. I have the perfect thing to match that dress." She turned her head and said, "Go grab a drink in the kitchen." The room was empty, so after pouring a glass of Coke and adding a shot of Rum, I sat down at the table for some peace and quiet for as long as I could get it.

Ashton strolled quietly into the room and relaxed into the seat next to me at the table. "Hey, kid, how you holding up?" He placed his hand on my arm in a consoling manner, but I moved it quickly away, not wanting to be coddled. "We need to stick together, bro. For our mom, for Katelyn, it's up to us to be strong." Pausing a moment, he glanced around. "I came in here to give you a heads up. MJ's here."

My head sprang up at the mention of her name. "What?" Without thinking, I jumped to my feet. Ashton grabbed my arm. "Let me go, I want to see her."

"There's something you should know first. It's important."

"Nothing's more important than me seeing her right now." Ashton's voice followed me as I swung the kitchen door outward to walk into the living room. Mary Jane was there and a man was helping her with her bag. As she turned to thank him, my eyes drifted to her extended belly. Calculating the time in my head, I determined we hadn't been together in over a year. She appeared to be at least seven or eight months along, which meant it didn't take her long to move on. Arm linked tightly through her companion's, I supposed he must be the father. I stayed out of sight for a moment as she introduced him to Gracie.

"Gracie, this is Tristan."

Tristan extended his hand to her, but she pulled him into a hug instead. "In this group, we're family and we hug, none of that handshaking nonsense." She winked at him, and all I could think was *Traitor*. As if she read my thoughts, Gracie saw me and offered an apologetic smile. Mary Jane turned to follow Gracie's gaze, and her face fell into a frown as her eyes met mine.

She approached cautiously. "Hi, Derrick. I'm so sorry about your father." She wrapped me in the warmth of a consoling hug. Out of habit, I nuzzled my nose against her neck, breathing in her sweet scent. She sighed contentedly in my ear. "I've missed you." Coming to my senses, I pushed her away gently. She turned and pulled her guy to stand beside her. "Tristan, this is Derrick."

Tristan extended his hand to me. "I've heard a lot about

you, Derrick." When I didn't shake his hand, he asked, "You want a hug too?"

"No, not really. I suppose congratulations are in order." Both wore confused expressions until I pointed at her swollen belly. Mary Jane's face paled as though she had forgotten she was wearing a bowling-ball-sized bump under her shirt. She opened her mouth, and I held my hand up. "Excuse me. I have to tend to our guests. You guys enjoy yourselves."

Enjoy yourselves? That was quite a response to give someone during a wake. Thinking straight was not in the cards for then. I couldn't be held accountable for anything I said. For that reason, I needed to go outside and be alone.

I grabbed a cold beer and moved toward the door, letting it slam behind me. Outside, I sat on a bench and began to scrape my fingers through my hair, trying to comprehend seeing the love of my life, not only with another man, but pregnant with his child. It hurt, badly, especially during that terrible time. How could she have sprung it on me like that? I wished she hadn't come at all. It would've hurt less than seeing her like that did. My thoughts were interrupted by the "guy" coming outside.

He stepped in front of me and extended his hand. "I'm sorry about your father." I shook his hand, reluctantly.

"Thanks. Sorry, I'm not usually as rude as I was in there." Why was I apologizing to this guy?

He chuckled and took a seat next to me. "There's not much I don't know about you."

"How's that?" Can't imagine my name came up much

in their pillow talk.

Tristan looked at me as though it was the dumbest question he'd heard. "MJ. You're pretty much everything she talks about. She misses you and Katelyn, a lot." It was my turn to offer the crazy look. He continued. "We're not together. We're only friends. That's all we've ever been. She's a fantastic girl and the best friend I've ever had."

I asked the question that had been killing me since I first saw her. "Aren't you the father of her baby?"

Tristan's forehead crinkled. "No. Wait, you don't know who the father is? I know what you're thinking, and what I'm about to say won't make much sense, but you're the only one she's been with."

I rolled my eyes and tried not to burst into laughter or lose my temper. "I'm not an idiot, and I can count. We haven't been together in over a year."

Tristan nodded. "You're right, you're not the father. Talk to her though, you'd be surprised at what you find out. It'll make you feel better."

He fidgeted for a moment, as though fighting with his thoughts. Then he said, "I shouldn't tell you this; it's not my place." He took a deep breath and said, "She's still in love with you. The moment Gracie called to tell her about your dad, she started calling for airline prices. She found out she couldn't fly in her third trimester and she panicked. She said she had to be there for you. She walked straight out to her car to start driving. That's why I'm here. I couldn't send her off on a ten-hour drive by herself, about to pop. I volunteered to drive us. She fidgeted the entire way here, worrying about what you would think when you saw her."

I sighed. "Why wouldn't she tell me she was pregnant?"

Tristan placed his hand on my shoulder. "Would you have heard her out on the phone with that kind of news?" I shook my head. He was right. I'd have hung up on her or zoned out for the rest of the conversation.

"Tristan, can you give us some time alone?" Mary Jane asked. She had stepped outside and was holding the door for Tristan as a hint to go back in. Nodding, he gave her a friendly kiss on the cheek as he passed. Waddling over to my side, she leaned back to take a seat next to me. "Sheesh, I'm the size of a whale," she said as she finally got comfortable, well, as comfortable as one could in her situation.

"You look even more beautiful than ever, exactly the way I imagined you would look pregnant one day." I glanced away and said softly, "Well, not exactly how I pictured it." She reached for my hand, and I stiffened and then relaxed at how normal it felt. "Tell me how this happened, MJ. Well, I know how it happened, but—"

She stopped me. "No, you don't. It isn't what you think. I haven't been intimate with anyone but you."

Rising to my feet, I let her hand drop to the bench. Angrily, I asked, "How is that possible?" Something occurred to me as I watched her rub her belly methodically. I kneeled in front of her, devastated at even the thought. "No, MJ, were you… was it…?" I couldn't bring myself to say the disgusting word.

Immediately reading my thoughts, she gasped, "No! No, it wasn't like what happened to Gracie. This was not an ugly thing." She cringed. "I hate telling you this today of all days. I wanted to be here for you. I didn't want to upset you. With everyone else knowing, I thought you already knew or that someone would warn you before I arrived. It was stupid of me to assume such a thing. I should've called and talked to you about it."

I relaxed. "Thank God. If that had happened to you…" I shook my head back and forth; there were no words to what I'd do for this girl if someone hurt her.

I closed my eyes as she caressed my cheek softly. "I love you, Derrick. Always have, always will. If I didn't, I wouldn't be here today springing this news on you."

Those words never hurt so much and felt so good at the same time. "Tell me who the father is," I pleaded.

"Remember our weekend in Atlanta?"

Of course, I remembered it. It was the last time I'd seen her in person, and it was our first time together. Instead of answering, I nodded so that she'd continue.

"There was more to that weekend than me wanting my first time to be with you and be special. Cameron had come to visit me a week or so before I called you. Gavin was going out of town, and they'd been having a rough time, so he didn't want to be alone. He broke down and told me they'd been trying to adopt and that everywhere they went, they were either shunned for being a gay couple or suddenly the meeting would take a completely awkward feel when the person realized they were the couple coming to sign up for adoption. His heart was broken and he was hurting so badly. I didn't know what to do. We started researching everything, and suddenly it dawned on me, surrogacy. All they needed was someone to carry a baby for them. In the middle of doing the research, he said to me, 'I wish I could find someone I trusted to do this. This seems so scary.' So, I offered myself as an option."

Moments of our trip in Atlanta suddenly made more sense as I listened to her story. "Cameron refused adamantly. He thanked me for considering it but knew I was a virgin and could never ask that of me. Cameron had been our hero for years, defending Gracie, Angel, and me to bullies, even when he paid the price. I had the chance to be a hero to him. Instead of arguing, I took matters into my own hands. Planning the trip to Atlanta was my way of pushing our relationship to the next step. Afterward, on our last day, I wanted to run the idea by you and see what you thought of me being a surrogate. We were supposed to make the plan together."

It didn't make sense why she never brought this up; we talked for weeks after that trip. "What changed in Atlanta, MJ?"

"Katelyn got sick. I distracted you from checking on her, and it ate away at me. Our relationship was straining the connection you'd built with your daughter. So, I told Cameron I wanted to be the surrogate after I ended our relationship."

None of this made sense to me. "Why didn't you tell me? Instead of breaking things off? You could have explained this all to me, and I might have understood. I'm almost positive I would have."

She laughed a soft chuckle. "You say that now because I'm as big as a house, and the deed is done. Watching Cameron suffer, knowing I could take away his pain was all too much. Knowing I might never get you back, I sacrificed us so he could be happy. You should've seen his face when the pregnancy test was positive. And the first ultrasound, it was a beautiful sight."

My eyes misted over with tears. This woman was even more amazing than I had ever dreamed. She continued. "I'm sorry. I wanted to tell you. Remember when you went to get your shower that last morning?" He nodded. "I told you I had something important to talk to you about. Then Gracie called about Katelyn being sick, and you needed to go, so I thought I would tell you later."

"Why didn't you tell me once she was better?"

"Cameron begged me to tell you, but it didn't seem right. I broke up with you because I was afraid you'd try to talk me out of it. Also, I thought it would be too confusing for Katelyn at the time. She's a smart girl, but that's a lot to take in for anyone."

"You're right. Katelyn wouldn't have understood. I wish you'd told me though, MJ. I heard you on the phone with Gracie…." The words trailed off. I was vulnerable and suddenly it hit me, my father was dead. My voice choked as my palm covered my mouth and I said, "My dad's dead."

Mary Jane pulled me into her arms as my body shook with all the emotions I'd bottled up inside ever since they told me he was gone. I'd not let it out once or accepted it as truth until that moment. Sitting there in the arms of the woman I loved, I wept until I felt like I had nothing left. At some point, she'd knelt in front of me to hold me. When I become conscious she was on the ground, I pulled away and helped her back up to a seat.

"Thank you," she said as she leaned back again. She held her arms out to me, and I lay my head against her stomach as she stroked my hair. We didn't say anything else to each other for the next few minutes. Feeling something brush against my cheek, I sat up. My eyes rolled up to meet hers, and they were closed. I rested my hand on her belly and felt the movement again, the baby kicking. She began to snore lightly, and I laughed, a foreign sound to me lately.

"Hey there, little one. You have a pretty strong kick."

The screen door opened, and Tristan stepped out onto the porch. He chuckled softly and gave me a teasing wink. "She fell asleep? She's so rude, isn't she?"

I stroked her face and said, "She's beautiful." Standing up, I embraced Tristan. He stiffened for a moment then returned the hug, patting my back. "Thank you for convincing me to listen. And thank you for taking care of her."

Tristan patted my back one more time and said, "It's my pleasure, man. Like I said, she's my best friend. I came out here because Gracie's looking for you. I think Ashton wants you to go somewhere with him."

Bending over, I pressed my lips gently against her forehead. "I hate to leave her when I just got her back. At least I think I did. I'm not really sure where we stand. I had a bit of a breakdown moment in the middle of our talk."

Tristan took my place beside her. "It's understandable,

man. She'll ask about you as soon as she wakes up. So, I'll keep her company till you come back."

Tipping my chin to him, I went back inside the house to track down Ashton.

CHAPTER THIRTEEN

MARY JANE

Waking up in an odd sleeping position on the swing, I placed my hand on my back as I tried to stretch out the kinks. Tristan sat beside me, playing on his cell phone. He glanced over as I adjusted my body into a more comfortable position. "Where's Derrick?"

"He had to run an errand with Ashton. You feel better after your nap?" Unable to remember when I fell asleep, I wondered if our conversation ended on a good note.

Then it hit me, and I smacked my palm against my forehead. "I'm such an asshole. I fell asleep while he was *literally* crying on my shoulder."

Giving a smirk, he replied, "He didn't seem to mind. He was curled up against your belly talking to the baby when I found him. Then he couldn't stop talking about how beautiful you are, so I'm pretty sure he wasn't bothered in the least."

Heat filled my cheeks. "Really?" With the screen door open, I heard the doorbell ring, interrupting our conversation. Since I knew Ashton and Gracie best, I went to answer it. A woman with auburn hair stood in the doorway holding a casserole dish.

"Oh, hello, I'm Lanie. I was dropping this off for the Collins family. Are you Gracie?" she asked with a disposition a little too cheery for visiting a grieving family.

Lanie. I recognized her name as the woman who answered Derrick's phone the other day. Friendly warmth emanated from her eyes and smile. She was quite pretty with her hair pulled up into a loose bun and her flawless complexion. "No, I'm Mary Jane, a friend of theirs. Come on in. They'll be back soon if you'd like to wait or I can tell them you dropped it off, whichever you feel comfortable with."

"I don't mind leaving it. So, Mary Jane? You're a friend of Derrick's too… right? We spoke on the phone?" Eyes dropping to my belly, she seemed more at ease. "When are you due?"

Wow, so many questions from this woman already. "Yes, I'm a friend of Derrick's. I'm due in a few weeks."

"You must be so excited to be a mom soon."

"I'm not keeping the baby. I'm only a surrogate for a friend." Not sure if my hormones were raging or this woman just hit every nerve I had, I tried to keep from losing my cool.

"Oh, okay, well that's strange," she said, scrunching up her face and looking away.

"How is that strange?" I asked, getting defensive with the woman who seemed to be making assumptions about me after we'd just met for the first time.

"You're so young. You're ruining your body for a friend and risking stretch marks and weight gain."

Nice choice for a date, Derrick. If he had a type, I hoped I never sounded as vapid as this woman did.

Reaching for the casserole, I bit my tongue to keep from saying anything crass. "I'll take that and let Ashton, Derrick, and Gavin know you brought it by. Have a nice day." Arms straight out in front of me, I waited for the dish to be placed in them. If she thought I was going to stand here while she insulted me, she had another think coming.

With a fake "I'm a popular girl, and I'm going to ruin your life" kind of smile, she said, "Tell Derrick I had a great time on our *second* date, and I hope to see him again very soon." Finally, she set the dish on my arms, adding a little weight as she did so.

"That's a real appropriate message to leave for a man who just lost his father."

Lanie realized her faux pas and began to retract her message when I slammed the door in her face. It wasn't the least bit mature, but I blamed my pregnancy hormones. When I slammed the casserole down on the kitchen table, I realized I wasn't alone in the house. Noise came from below in the basement rec room. Glancing outside, I could still see Tristan on his phone. Nervously, I crept to the door to listen to what was happening downstairs. The loud crash below scared me, causing me to stumble backward a step. I squeaked out a scream of fright at the noise, and it was answered by a male voice. "Hello? Who's up there?"

Footsteps grew louder as someone bounded up the stairs. I turned to run to the back door when I heard a familiar voice. "Mary Jane?"

Spinning around, I grabbed my chest and breathed a sigh of relief. "Gavin, you scared me half to death. I thought Tristan and I were the only ones here, and he's outside."

"I'm so sorry, MJ. I thought I was alone here too." Gavin embraced me, then bent down to kiss my belly. "I hope I didn't rattle my sweet girl too much."

"She's fine. I think she's as relieved to hear her daddy's voice as I am." His face was streaked with tears. I lifted Gavin's hand, noticing several new scratches along his knuckles as well. "What happened?"

Emotional turmoil brewed inside him as his face scrunched with his warring reactions. "I've been trying to be strong for Ashton and Derrick, but it's so hard. I know he wasn't my biological dad, but he was better to me than my parents ever were."

"Sweetie," I whispered, unsure of what I could say to comfort him. It occurred to me what was happening. Gavin came out to his family in high school and they kicked him out. The Collins family took him into their home and accepted him as one of their own. Craig Collins was his father as much as he was Derrick and Ashton's. "Would you like to talk about it?"

Taking a seat on the couch, he lifted my feet up into his lap and tossed my shoes to the floor. "You look exhausted, MJ, so let me do this for you while I talk."

"No arguments from me. Talk to me, Gav."

"When I told my parents that I was gay, they spouted every Bible verse they could think of in my face. As far as they were concerned, I might as well screw animals. Living my life this way was no better than being a pedophile or a rapist."

For anyone who'd suffered through such pain of simply being themselves, my heart ached. He continued. "Ashton got up in my father's face in my defense. It was amazing of him. I'd known he was good for Addison, my sister, but I didn't know what a truly amazing person he was until that day." I'd heard about Addison once or twice.

"Ashton told me I could stay with him, but I insisted his parents be told the truth so they would know the kind of person I was. Ashton tried to argue, of course, telling me there was nothing wrong with me, but I was set on what I wanted. Prepared for his family to berate me as well, I walked in with my guard up. Sitting quietly, I listened as he explained to his parents how I came out to mine and they kicked me out. You know what his father said?"

No one had ever told me this much of Gavin's story before. "He said, 'Welcome to the family, son. Let's take you upstairs and show you your room.' Never once did he say anything negative to me. Every holiday, every birthday I had from that moment on, I received the exact same treatment as Derrick and Ashton. We were brothers, blood be damned. You know I went to him to ask his opinion on proposing to Cameron. His eyes filled with tears as he told me how proud he was I wanted to take such a huge step in my life. He said he thought Cameron and I made an amazing couple and we'd be lifers. Then, when we told him we were pregnant, he was astounded. He said, 'Two grandbabies in one year, what a blessing.' He *was* my dad. I miss him...." His voice trailed off.

As I pulled him close, he rested his head on my shoulder, sniffing back tears every few moments. "What happened to your hand, Gavin?" I asked after a few moments of silence.

"One of the walls downstairs is brick; I thought I'd have a fist fight with it to relieve some of my anger without damaging the house." His knuckles were cracked and bleeding with bits of dirt.

"That's not like you. You're lucky you didn't do more than scratch it up," I said. Gavin had been the calm one of the group. He wasn't flamboyant like Cameron or temperamental like Gracie. Even Ashton had his moments of anger in the past, but never Gavin. "Let's clean your hand up." I led him to the bathroom where I tended to his cuts while he continued venting.

"This is the first time I've lost someone close to me since Addison. I'm tired of losing the important people in my life." His hand soaking wet but clean, I grabbed a towel to wrap around it.

"Feel." I placed his hand on my belly as the baby began to kick. "Did you feel it?"

The light in his eyes returned; his smile illuminated his

face as he bent to my tummy. "Hey, baby girl, Daddy's here."

I had a lot of discomforts, inconveniences, and bodily functions with this pregnancy, which caused me days of regret and worry I'd made a mistake. Then moments with Cameron or Gavin, seeing how excited they were to meet their daughter, made it all worth it. The little person who he'd never laid eyes on was able to help ease the pain for him that I couldn't.

Kneeling in front of me, a hand on each side of my stomach, he began to sing to the baby. He didn't notice the door open behind him; Cameron, Gracie, Ashton, and Derrick stepped inside and quietly listened to the expectant father serenading his child. Cameron's eyes grew misty with tears of joy. He knelt next to Gavin, who smiled when he noticed him. A sweet kiss was shared before Cameron placed his hand on my stomach to feel the flutters too.

***

The funeral the next day was a beautiful tribute to Craig's life and his family. Ashton wrote a eulogy, but it was read by Gracie because he'd been too emotional to speak. Afterward, we all went back to Ashton and Gracie's for a private celebration of his life.

Everyone but Derrick and I went downstairs to the rec room. We told them we'd join them in a few minutes. "Are you hungry?" Derrick asked.

"Starving actually." I rubbed my stomach. "This one is

hungry pretty much all the time. Luckily, I haven't had any horribly strange cravings."

Derrick spotted the casserole on the counter as soon as we stepped into the kitchen. He inspected it and said, "This looks interesting. It's always weird to me the custom of people bringing food to funerals. Wonder who brought this by?"

Trying to control my annoyance, I rolled my eyes but kept my voice calm. "Oh yeah, Lanie stopped by and left it for you."

Derrick stiffened and without looking at me said, "We only went out twice, MJ. It meant nothing to me. The first time was coffee and talking, mostly about Katelyn. The second was the other night. We never even shared a kiss. I explained to her there wouldn't be a third date because I had feelings for someone else." If I could've jumped up and down right then without giving birth, I might've even done a cartwheel I was so happy to hear those details.

Keeping up the nonchalance, I said, "You have nothing to explain to me, Derrick. I called you the night you were out with her. She answered your phone, and I assumed it was a date by what she said. I wasn't sure until now though."

"You called me?" Pulling his cell phone out of his pocket, he went through his phone log. "Why didn't she tell me you called? Did you tell her not to?"

"No. In fact, I told her to tell you I called. It doesn't matter right now. Let's eat something," I said as my stomach rumbled. Not sure if it was hunger or nausea over the topic of conversation.

"Would you like some of this?" he asked, holding up the pan.

"No, definitely not," I said, sounding more disgusted than I meant to.

"What's wrong? Is it because of Lanie? What did she say to you, MJ?"

"Forget it, it's nothing," I said, waving it off. "It looks pretty tasty. Maybe we could try it."

Derrick walked in front of me, trapping me between the counter and himself. "Tell me," he said as his hand moved up to stroke my cheek. Licking my lips, I stared into his eyes, hoping he'd kiss me.

Unable to breathe, or move, or think with him so close to me, my heart raced. Instead of answering or waiting for him, I leaned forward and captured his lips with mine. It had been almost a year since I kissed this man, and I missed it more than I realized. Pressing me against the counter, intensifying the kiss, his response was exactly what I hoped.

Fireworks exploded, beautiful music played, the camera moved around us in slow motion—so there was no camera, but we put the ending of *Pretty Woman* to shame with our kiss. As I opened my mouth to catch a breath, Derrick took the opportunity to slip his tongue inside. I moaned against his mouth, making him press into me harder. We were broken apart by the baby kicking.

Derrick chuckled and patted my belly. "Sorry about that, kid." Grinning as he cradled my stomach, I noticed the smile slowly fading from his lips before he dropped his hands into his pockets.

"I shouldn't have done that, I'm sorry," I said, backing out of reach.

"What? Why?" Derrick asked befuddled.

"You look upset."

Pulling me back into his arms, he smirked. "Yeah, because I hated that so much."

He moved toward me, and I pulled away before he kissed me again. "Why the long face a minute ago?"

Clearing his throat, he sighed. "I'd imagined your swollen, pregnant belly many times, feeling the kicks, the flutters, the movements of our child. I never imagined you carrying another man's baby. It hurts, MJ. I keep telling myself you are doing a good thing, reminding myself sex was not involved. But looking at you, it breaks my heart."

"It was too much for me to come here, wasn't it? Too soon?"

Grasping my hands in his, our fingers intertwined. "No. I couldn't have gotten through today without seeing your face. You give me strength."

"Tell me about Lanie. How did you meet her? What was the relationship like?"

"No relationship, sweetheart. Like I said, we went out twice. She's Katelyn's teacher, and she flirted with me during a vulnerable time and I asked her out." All but spitting the words out, he moved toward my mouth once more.

"Well, she seemed as though she really wanted to prove you were more when she dropped off her casserole."

Derrick relented, backing away and sighing in defeat. "What did she say? Please, tell me."

"I'm sorry. It was childish of me to say anything about her. She was marking her territory is all. I think she felt threatened by me. It's not important."

Derrick sighed once more, closing his eyes. "How she treats my friends is definitely important to me."

"Is that what we are? Friends?" I asked, hoping to elicit a discussion about us. It was selfish, I knew. The time wasn't right to get into a full discussion about us, though I couldn't help but be curious after the toe-tingling kiss.

"You tell me where we stand, because I don't know anymore. I want you in my life. I've wanted nothing but you for the last two years. Then you pushed me away. Now you show up on my doorstep pregnant with my brother's child. It's a lot to take in." His words stung deep.

"Don't say it that way. You know I'm a surrogate only." Hurt as he was, I couldn't let him twist this around into something ugly.

"It's still a lot for a guy to process," Derrick stated matter-of-factly.

"Is it because of the toll it will take on my body? You're worried you won't find me attractive?"

His look of confusion turned to one of disgust. "Is that what she said? Did Lanie suggest I wouldn't find you attractive now?"

"I don't think she meant it that way. I think it's my hormones."

"What did she say exactly?" Derrick pleaded once more for an answer.

"She thought it was strange I wanted to destroy my body

for a baby who isn't mine. And she made a point of letting me know you'd been on two dates." Biting my lip, I wished I had kept my mouth shut. I'd met Lanie once. It wasn't fair of me to judge her based on a first impression.

Changing the subject was the easiest way out of this. "Gavin needs you right now. He's taking your father's death rough. He's been forcing himself to be strong for you and Ash, but he's breaking. He needs his brothers around him."

"I'm not sure I can help him. I haven't come to terms with it myself," Derrick said, his gaze dropping to the floor in shame.

With my index finger, I lifted his chin so he'd make eye contact with me and said, "Then help each other. Spend the next few weeks doing brother stuff, reminiscing about your dad, family dinners, whatever it takes. When this little one comes into the world, Gavin will be busy with daddy duties himself. Take this time for you. I have three months left of my internship, around two months left of pregnancy, and then I'll be coming home. We can figure out us at that time."

"So, that's it? You're going to leave again?" His stance became rigid, his tone harsh.

"You knew I wasn't home for good, Derrick. This is a time you need to be with family."

"I thought we were family. You always say that about your friends, does that not include me anymore?" Derrick asked, sounding dejected.

Gracie appeared in the kitchen doorway. She glanced from Derrick's sad face to mine, then asked, "Are you two all right?"

"Ask her, I haven't got a clue," Derrick said as he turned and left.

Gracie stepped forward. "What happened?"

"He lost his dad."

"I mean between the two of you," she replied.

"I know. Right now there is too much grief in his heart for there to be a discussion about the two of us. He needs to cope with this loss first."

"Maybe you can help him—"

I cut her off. "Drop it, Gracie. Please. I'm only here a few more days. How about a girls' day tomorrow like old times?"

Tristan walked in at that moment and said, "Mind if I crash girls' day?"

Gracie wrapped her arm through his. "We don't mind at all. Cameron lets us give him makeovers when he crashes. Are you up for some nail polish and hair dye?"

He eased out of Gracie's grasp. "On second thought, maybe I'll hang out here and watch a movie."

Gracie laughed and bumped her hip against his. "No worries, Tristan. We won't torture you that way. Of course, you should come with us." She gave a fleeting look to the door of the kitchen and then whispered, "I want the guys to spend some time together, so I'm going to convince Cameron to leave Gavin's side to join us as well. I think it would be good for the three brothers."

"Great minds think alike," I said to her. "Go get Cameron, and let's make plans."

Chapter Fourteen

DERRICK

Mary Jane was right, even though I hated to admit it. I needed to get through this with my brothers before she and I started a relationship again, if we decided to. I knew it was what I wanted; she was all I wanted. I wasn't sure she felt the same about me anymore; though the kiss we shared gave me a problem that couldn't be handled around my brothers. A few deep breaths and thoughts of anything but Mary Jane helped me relax.

Ashton, Gavin, and I were going to rent a boat to go fishing and drink a toast to Dad. We drove up to Dale Hollow Lake in Byrdstown, Tennessee, only two hours away, where we'd spent many camping trips with our dad.

We left in the early morning so we could enjoy a full day. We stopped first to rent a boat. While Ashton paid for the rental, Gavin and I gathered the fishing supplies from Ash's truck. "Let's drop these in the boat once Ashton gets the keys, and then we'll head over to the convenience store and pick up some snacks and a couple of six-packs." Gavin nodded silently in agreement, he was quiet most of the ride up. As I rested my hand on his shoulder, he peered up at me. "He was really proud of you, Gav. I'm sorry your daughter won't get to meet him."

Gavin smiled. "Thanks, Derrick." He pointed toward the convenience store. "I think I'll go grab those snacks and drinks, man. I'll be back."

Ashton headed over, waving the keys. "Time to get going." He looked around and said, "Where's Gav?"

"He went to get the snacks to save us time. You load up, and I'll wait for him here." I was sure he volunteered mostly to avoid becoming emotional. Mentioning his unborn child never meeting our dad had brought tears to his eyes.

Gavin came out of the store a moment later with his hands full, so I ran to meet him. "Ashton's got the boat ready for us. I'm looking forward to a few of these." I held up the six-packs for clarification.

Once out on the boat, we all assumed our lounging positions with a beer in one hand and a fishing pole in the other. "So, I've taken Gracie fishing before. Either of you going to take your significant others fishing to keep up tradition?" Ashton asked.

I laughed softly. "Tradition? Dad took Mom once and she hated it. She thought it was cruel to lure them in with food just to kill them."

Ashton replied, "Yeah but when it came to Dad's fried catfish dinners, she wasn't complaining then!" We all laughed at the comical hypocrisy. Ashton turned to Gavin. "You going to bring Cameron to fish sometime?"

Gavin let out a big hearty laugh. "I love the man, but he'd never in a million years go fishing. In some ways, I think he created the gay stereotype himself. That man's idea of roughing it is to stay in a 3-star hotel."

Ashton and I laughed at how true his statement sounded for Cameron's personality, and then I asked, "How did you two fall for each other? You're so different."

Gavin smiled reminiscently. "He makes me laugh. He has the biggest heart of anyone I've ever met. It doesn't hurt that he's hot either."

Ashton replied, "I can easily see that. If I were gay, I could see me falling for Cameron. When I first met him, I thought he was over the top, but the more you're around him, you can't help but love the guy." He turned to me. "What about you, D? Are you going to take MJ fishing?"

Saved by the pull of my fishing line, I reeled in a nice large bass. It was as long as my arm, so not a bad size at all.

"You should bring MJ here, Derrick," Ashton said, pressing the subject once again.

"I'm not sure there will ever be anything between MJ and me again, Ash. She wants me to take time away from her to deal with Dad's death. For her internship, she asked me to move on. Then she pulled me back in to drop me again to have a baby and lie to me about it. Her actions don't seem to display any hope for the future with me. Every time we get together, she pushes me away again."

Saying it out loud was the first time I thought it all through and came to that conclusion. Everything Mary Jane had done in her life had kept us apart; perhaps it was what she was trying to tell me. After a few minutes of quiet, Gavin spoke up, "What MJ did for us, I can never repay the sacrifice she made. Don't hold it against her, Derrick, for not telling you about it. We tried to talk her out of it. That girl has a heart of gold."

Knowing Mary Jane as I did, everything he said was valid, and I couldn't deny it.

"She's putting her body through hell to give Cameron and me a child we may never have been able to have any other way. And it's Cameron's biological child, which is even more amazing for us. She loves you, and she put her dreams of a life with you on hold, possibly permanently, to make this sacrifice. She's something special."

My stomach clenched with different emotions: anger, grief, heartache, but most of all, love. "She's definitely amazing. I'm not holding anything against her. She's the most unselfish person I know. All I'm saying is she doesn't seem interested in being with me, and I don't want to push her."

Gavin clicked his tongue and then asked, "What about Lanie? Anything there holding you two up?"

I scoffed. "Hardly. She's cool, not bad looking, and we had an okay date the other night, but there wasn't much chemistry there, for my part at least."

"You think she felt more?" Ashton asked.

Shrugging, I said, "Maybe. MJ said she was a bit catty when she dropped food by the house." Sighing, I admitted the other issue. "Besides, she's Katelyn's teacher, and it almost seems wrong to pursue her. Katelyn doesn't know we went out though, and I have no plans to tell her. I want to keep my dates off her radar so she doesn't grow attached. MJ was one who couldn't be helped."

Ashton nudged me with his elbow. "I still think you guys will work things out."

"You think Mom's going to be okay? They were married a long time. She seems to be holding up all right, I guess," I said, staring off into the clear water, purposely changing the subject from my love life.

Shrugging his shoulders, Ashton replied, "It doesn't seem to have hit her yet. Gracie's been checking on her for me while I made all the arrangements. Autumn seems to keep her occupied and strong."

"We shouldn't have left her alone today," I said, wishing we'd included her in our trip down memory lane.

"She's got her two sisters, Aunt Miranda and Aunt Iris. She'll be fine. You know how those women are when they get together." Rolling my eyes, I thought about the cheek pinching and questions the aunts would have if we were around, and I felt thankful for the reprieve.

The song "Rainbow Connection" started playing on Gavin's phone. Ashton smirked. "Did Cameron choose that to be funny?"

Grinning with a nod, Gavin answered his phone. "Hey, babe, are you having a good time with the girls?" Gavin laughed at whatever Cameron's response was, then said, "Yeah, we're doing as well as can be expected. Just having a few beers and fishing out on the boat. The guys said you should come along sometime."

Gavin pushed the speakerphone button when Cameron responded, "Honey, you know you ain't ever getting me to hold any fishing pole or go anyway near a body of water with a creature of any kind in it. I need an indoor pool with hot lifeguards to save me if I pretend to drown for attention."

Gavin gave us a look of "I told you so" before responding, "I know. It never hurts to ask."

"You boys have fun now, love you, Gav," Cameron said with a kissing noise before Gavin took him off speakerphone and said, "Love you."

Ashton sighed. "It's peaceful out here. Don't get me wrong, I love my daughter more than life itself, but sometimes I need a break from the crying."

"You're preaching to the choir, man. You're lucky you have Gracie, but I was lucky I had Mom and Dad to help me too. I miss Katelyn every second I'm away from her, but I still need a break even now. She has gotten so girly lately." I pointed at Gavin. "I blame your husband."

With a smile of sympathy, Gavin replied, "I know. I am going to have a handful with him and our daughter striving to be fabulous all the time." He reeled in his line and then set his pole beside him on the floor of the boat. He ran his fingers through his faux hawk and said, "She's never going to know the man who saved my life." Ashton and I followed suit, reeling our lines in to sit back and let Gavin speak.

Gavin's face reddened with anger. "After all the pain and suffering, I lose the only father I've ever really had in a freak accident only a few weeks before my child is born? What makes this fair?"

Gavin stood up, moved to the side of the boat, and began to heave over the edge of it, losing the contents of his lunch as he released more emotions. He had placed his phone on silent, and it was buzzing now. Ashton went to comfort Gavin while I answered his phone. "Hey, Cameron. Gavin's fine, he's having a moment right now, but I'll have him call you back. I promise you, he's in good hands."

When I turned, Gavin had collapsed against the boat with his back against the wall, knees pulled up to his chest, head resting on his knees. Ashton knelt in front of him with a bottle of water. "Let it all out, Gavin. You know you're not judged by us."

Gavin took a swig from the water bottle, closed the top, and set it down. He waved me over. I took the empty floor space beside him, and he put one arm around my neck and pulled Ashton in to wrap his other arm around him. We sat with our heads together as if in a football huddle. "I love you guys. You really are my brothers, even though it seems like a creep factor since Ashton dated my sister." We all three laughed at his inappropriately timed but much-needed humor. "Seriously, I'd be shit without you."

"Your breath smells like shit from puking," I said jokingly. He responded by blowing air in my face, then laughing as we pulled apart from each other. "Let's get the hell up off this boat and go home. I think I need to carpe diem before it's too late," I said.

Ashton grinned, then headed to the driver's seat. "I hope that means what I think it means."

It took an hour to get back to the dock, pack up our gear, then get on the road. Two hours later, we were back at Ashton's house. Anxiously I ran in the door to find Mary Jane, but found the house was empty. A dry-erase board on the fridge had a note "Gone out for Chinese, be back soon." So, I sat down to wait for the girl of my dreams to walk back in that door so I could grab life by the balls the way my dad always did.

CHAPTER FIFTEEN

MARY JANE

Our day of fun with Tristan and Cameron turned into an afternoon of bonding. We were only out for a few hours; we went to paint pottery together. Afterward, we picked up some wine and went back to Ash and Gracie's. They drank wine while I slipped my shoes off and propped up my swollen feet.

"Aw, baby girl, do your feet hurt?" Cameron asked, sliding over to rest beside me.

"They look like stuffed sausages, so yeah, you could say they hurt. I'm retaining water like crazy but also peeing more times a day than Cameron looks in the mirror."

Gracie gasped. "Wow, that's a lot of peeing." We all laughed, except Cameron who politely flipped me off.

"Want me to rub your feet?" Tristan asked.

"Ooh, girl. You should keep this one around if he's willing to do that kind of stuff without getting laid. It's all right though, Tristud, I'll take care of my baby momma today. I never get to pamper her, nor did I think I'd ever say those words," Cameron said, shaking his head.

He started to rub my feet. At first I cringed at the pain; then the more he rubbed, the better they felt. I put my head back and began to moan in pleasure. Cameron cleared his throat. "Whew, honey. I never thought I'd make a woman make those noises."

Tristan and Gracie went to the kitchen to grab a few snacks for the four of us. While they were gone, Cameron started in with a deep, meaningful talk. "So, Derrick knows about the baby now. Are you two going to work through things?"

"I don't know. He deserves better than me, Cam."

"Why would you say that? Who could be better than you?" Cam asked sincerely.

"Anyone." I sat up, putting my feet back on the ground. Cameron moved to sit next to me, placing his arm on the back of the couch behind my shoulders and turning so that his body faced me. "I keep pushing him away. Yesterday, I pulled him in for a passionate, intense kiss only to pull away a moment later and tell him it isn't the right time for us to be together."

Cameron placed his hand under his chin and leaned forward with a grin. "Tell me more about this passionate, intense kiss." He winked at me, then reached forward to run his fingers through my hair. "Sweetie, you're scared. You and Derrick had a short but powerful relationship. You two have been through crazy things most couples do not have to deal with. The man was shot saving your life and the lives of your friends. You're pregnant with his brother-in-law's baby, which is like a Jerry Springer moment no couple needs."

I tossed my head back in frustration but gave a faint laugh. "Stop saying it like that."

Cameron scooted closer, resting his head on my shoulder. "I was trying to make you smile. Seriously though, what you did for Gavin and me… well, you are the real definition of fabulous in my book."

"It's been my pleasure. Seeing how happy you two have been for each new moment of this pregnancy has been worth it for me." Changing the subject on him, I said, "In a few weeks, you are going to be a dad. How do you feel?"

"What if she hates me? What if she hates both of us? What if people are mean to her because she has two dads? The closer it gets, the more I grow terrified I'm going to ruin her life."

"Call Gavin and talk to him about it." I grabbed his cell phone off the table, found Gavin in the contacts under "Hubby," and hit Send.

He took the phone from me and sat up. Sounding confused, he asked, "Um… Derrick? Hey, where's Gavin?" He sat up straighter with panic on his face. "Is he all right? Do I need to be there?" Relaxing a little, he said, "Thanks for taking care of him. I'll call him later."

"Everything okay with Gavin?" I asked.

"Derrick said he was having a moment. He said they've got him taken care of though. I know Ash and Derrick will make sure he's fine. He has a lot to deal with right now. I will rely on my girls to help me through my fatherhood worries for a moment."

"You're right," I said. His words resonated in my head, reminding me I needed to give Derrick time to deal with his father's death. Sitting up, I slipped my shoes back on as Tristan and Gracie came back into the living room. "Tristan, can we talk a minute?"

Gracie spoke up. "We were thinking about going to get Chinese for dinner. So don't be gone long."

I dragged Tristan back to Gracie's room and shut the door. "Are you up to driving back tonight?"

Tristan's brow crinkled. "Why? What did I miss?"

"Nothing. Derrick and I can't keep going around and around about whether we have a relationship or not. He has more important things happening right now."

"Stop and think for a minute, MJ. I know you're worried about him, but you're the one person who could make him face this loss by being here. Do you really think running off without saying goodbye is going to help him?" Tristan had a good point. If there was any chance for us when I came home, I needed to at least say goodbye to Derrick and not run off with my tail between my legs.

Gracie was in the kitchen writing a note to Ashton on their dry erase board. "Hey, girl, I'm starving. I thought we could pick Autumn up on the way to grab some dinner."

"Sounds good to me." Wrapping my arm around her

shoulders, I leaned my head against Gracie's.

"You okay, sweets?" asked Gracie.

"Yep. It just feels good to be home. Tomorrow when Derrick gets back, it's going to be hard to say goodbye again."

"You'll be back home in no time. And I have faith you and Derrick will work through everything. You two are made for each other." She squeezed my shoulder and I smiled. How come everyone else was so sure of a happily ever after for us, yet I was terrified it would never happen?

"From your lips." In need of a subject change before I broke down in tears, I stated, "Let's go get some food. I'm starving."

On the way to the restaurant, my text alert went off.

Derrick: When you guys get back from dinner, I want to talk. I'll wait for you at Gracie and Ash's.

He was waiting for me? "Derrick's at the house waiting for me. He wants to talk. What do you think it means?"

"Only one way to know. You can skip dinner and take the car back to talk to him. You two could use a little alone time."

Me: We haven't made it to dinner yet.

Derrick: Ashton's on his way there with Gavin. Can you come back to talk?

Gracie had no problem with me taking her car back. She texted Ashton to let him know, took the car seat out for the ride back, and tossed me the keys.

Me: On my way.

Derrick: See you soon, sweetheart

Nothing made me smile more than when he called me sweetheart.

On the way back to the house, I went over everything I wanted to say. When I stepped up to the doorway and saw Derrick's face, my mind went blank. "Hi." One word was all I could muster.

Derrick chuckled softly. "Hi. Come on in." Passing him in the doorway, a whiff of his cologne hit my nose. My favorite scent, one I would never forget.

"How was the trip? You're back early, right?"

"Yeah. We worked through a lot of emotional stuff we'd been holding in. Especially Gavin." Reaching out, Derrick took my hand in his. "I don't want things to be awkward between us."

"I'm ashamed to admit I almost left tonight, without saying goodbye. Tristan convinced me to stay."

"Why?"

"It's not important. What did you want to talk about?" Bringing up my insecurities would get us nowhere. It was best to let Derrick do the talking.

"First I wanted to thank you for dropping everything to be with me. It means more than you know. I'm not sure I could've gotten through the funeral without you here." With a squeeze of my hand, he gave me a smile with misty eyes. "With that being said, I want us to have a real shot. I'm not going to hound you about it or force you to make a decision right this second. But, until you move back home, I want you to think about us and what you want."

Running my hand over my belly methodically, I listened to everything he said. "In the meantime?"

"Time and space to think for both of us. We can text once in a while if you'd like, but for the most part, we'll wait until you move back home."

"I think I can agree to those terms." It was something at least—a glimpse of hope for a future, something I wasn't sure of before with the looming presence of his date with Lanie.

When he extended his hand, I gave him an odd look. "Shake on it?" I chuckled and grasped his hand. Our eyes locked, and the sparks were still between us.

That night I slept better than I had in weeks, and on the drive home to Florida, I relayed everything to Tristan who wouldn't stop gloating about how right he was for me not to run off without talking to Derrick.

***

In May, the baby came, a month before the internship had ended. Cameron and Gavin flew down the minute Tristan called them to tell them I was in labor. Only minutes before their baby girl made her debut, they ran into the room, all suited up in scrubs ready to support me.

Cameron was the first one to hold her, so I'm told. Labor was not progressing fast enough for a safe delivery, so they took me in for an emergency C-section. Tristan held my hand, never leaving my side. His face was the first one I saw when I woke up. A moment later, they brought the baby in the room to let me see her. Gavin asked if I wanted to hold her, and I thought it would be rude to say no. The moment they placed her in my arms, I began to cry.

Addison Grace was beautiful and looked like a mixture of Cameron and me. At first, my emotions from holding the baby made me think I'd never be able to give her up. Then I saw Gavin take her back, and the joy on his and Cameron's face overwhelmed me. I knew they were her parents.

"We can never thank you enough for this little girl, MJ." Gavin bent down to kiss my forehead. "The best way we could think of is to have you be her godmother. Will you do us the honor?"

Tears spilled down my cheek as I replied, "It would be my pleasure."

His gaze fixed on the baby, Cameron said, "One day we'll tell her all about the amazing gift you gave us."

Gracie, Ashton, and Angel came to the hospital to see all of us. They'd left Autumn with Ashton's mom for a few days so they could come. I kept watching the door, waiting for Derrick, but he didn't show up. Our agreement was no communication, but I needed him to help me get through this. For the time being, I'd have to rely on my other friends. Gracie stepped over to my side and whispered, "How are you?"

"Hanging in there. She's beautiful, and I know she's not mine, but this is so much harder than I thought it would be."

Angel stepped up next to me. "I found us a house to rent in Nashville. We'll be moving home soon."

On the last day of my internship with Disney, I still hadn't made a decision about taking the full-time position. It was a fantastic opportunity, one I'd dreamt about for many years. The problem was I'd have to stay in Florida, away from everyone. It was a lot to consider. They gave me some leeway since I had just given birth. If I wanted the job, it would be here for me in three months when I was ready to start.

After weighing the pros and cons, moving backing home seemed best. As long as I could find a comparable job in Nashville, it was where I wanted to be. It was home.

Soon we'd be back in Nashville where I could finally see what would happen when I came face to face with Derrick again.

Angel was packing up the apartment when I walked through the door. She stepped into the living room wearing shorts that left nothing to the imagination with a tank top. "Damn, girl. You need to put some clothes on. Tristan's coming over to help pack in a few."

Angel shook her hips. "If you got it, flaunt it—" Then she smacked her right hip. "—and I've been told I got it." She laughed, then lifted the box off the kitchen counter, taped it down with duct tape, and wrote kitchen in all caps with a Sharpie.

Tristan knocked once before popping his head inside. "Hello, ladies…." His voice trailed off, and I saw why when I looked over to see him staring at Angel, who was bent forward filling a box, giving him a full view of her cleavage. Angel looked up and gave him a smile before standing up, turning to her bedroom, then giving him something to watch as she swayed her hips until she was out of sight.

Clearing my throat, I said teasingly, "Are you done ogling my friend now?"

"Um… I wasn't… uh… I'm here to pack?" he said it as a question, hoping maybe it was the right answer for the time being. I laughed and motioned for him to join me in the kitchen. Tristan began packing up our cabinet full of coffee mugs. He paused when he saw one of them. Holding it up to me, he asked, "Who made this for you? It's adorable."

"Katelyn. I used it every day when I first moved here. Then after Derrick and I broke up, I hid it in the back because it was too difficult to look at it."

"Have you talked to him?"

"Nope. I'm sure Gracie or Ashton have told him I'm moving back," I said.

When moving day arrived, Tristan had us packed up in the truck in less than two hours. He was moving back with us, and we were going to live in a three-bedroom house not far from the neighborhood Gracie lived in. I offered to share a room with Macy, but Tristan insisted he'd share a closet with her and sleep on the couch so that each of us girls had our own rooms. Tristan pulled his car behind the moving van and Angel and I rode in mine.

When Tristan brought up the idea of moving to Macy, she reacted much better than he expected. She was genuinely excited about the opportunity of going to a new school.

There were a lot of bad memories for both Macy and Tristan in Florida. A new start was what they both wanted.

Leaving their mom behind would be the hardest part. Her Alzheimer's had progressed so much she didn't recognize them anymore when they visited. Tristan decided he would have the hospital keep in touch with him, and I heard him call the nurse once in a while too, but it was too hard on them to visit her anymore. Even the doctor said she wouldn't know the difference; plus, it could make her stressed.

The ten-hour drive went by quicker than I expected. When we pulled up to the house, we had a welcoming committee. Gracie, Ashton, and Autumn had gotten the keys for our place and set up a nice dinner to welcome us home. After exchanging hugs and taking a few moments to play with baby Autumn, Ashton and Tristan unloaded the couch so we could have somewhere to sit.

I walked back out to the truck to grab a few things when Ashton pulled me aside. "Hey, I wanted to ask you a favor."

"Sure, Ash. What's up?"

"Katelyn wants to see you. She asked me the other day, and I promised I'd find a way. Tomorrow afternoon she'll be coming to our house. I was hoping you could meet me at the park and surprise her?"

"I'd love to. Just text me and let me know which park and when."

Later in the evening, I had a text to meet him at two in the park where I'd first met Derrick and Katelyn.

I arrived early to meet Ashton, anxious to see Katelyn

after so long. They hadn't arrived yet, so I sat down on a swing to wait. As my mind drifted off into memories, a voice brought me out of my daydream. "Would you like a push?"

Standing behind me with a grin on his face and a pink carnation in his hand was Derrick.

"What are you doing here?"

CHAPTER SIXTEEN

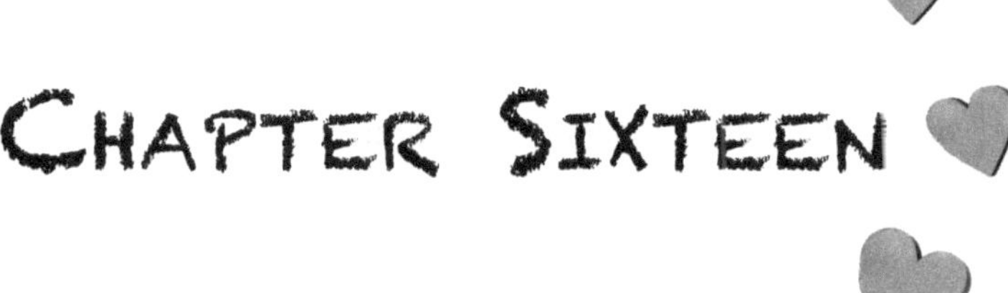

DERRICK

After Mary Jane and I had talked at Ashton's, I wanted to beg her to stay. Many times I considered texting her, telling her how I felt, begging her to come back to me, but I wanted it to be her decision. Apparently, absence made the heart grow fonder, and I suppose I wanted to test the theory. Keeping my distance had been incredibly difficult.

When Gracie called to tell me Mary Jane was in labor, it took all the strength I had not to go down there to see her. They texted me pictures, and Ashton gave me a play by play of everything he could, so much so it was almost as good as being there.

Then when Ashton told me the date Mary Jane was moving back, I asked him to help me speak to her. We hadn't spoken since the day she left after my father's funeral.

almost three months ago. Going through him seemed the most logical way to ensure she'd show up. No matter what her decision would be about us, I wanted to know.

My plan worked because I was sitting in my car, watching her walk toward the swings. She looked beautiful as the sunlight brightened her blonde hair and danced across her skin. She was wearing a light pink T-shirt that gave the illusion of being sheer. Her denim shorts hugged her curvy hips and left her long legs exposed, ending with a pair of summer sandals.

Swinging gently as she stared off into space unaware of my admiration of her, I wondered what was in her mind. Being in the place we first met, I hoped her mind was full of fond memories. Gathering my courage, I grabbed the pink carnation off the passenger seat of my truck and made my way over to her. She didn't hear me approach from behind because she never turned around.

"Would you like a push?" I asked, causing her to turn.

As her eyes met mine, her mouth dropped open in surprise and she said, "What are you doing here?"

My mind couldn't function enough to find the words to answer her. Handing her the pink carnation, I simply smiled. As she returned my smile, my shoulders relaxed.

"I'd love a push."

For a few moments, I pushed her on the swing and we didn't speak. It was just a moment of peace before the serious talk I knew would follow.

"I assume this was a setup and Katie isn't coming?" she asked, letting her feet hit the ground to come to a stop. I grabbed her hips to slow her down in a gentler manner.

With my hands on her hips and my face close to hers, I inhaled the sweet smell of her subtle perfume and gently placed a soft kiss atop her shoulder blade. "Are you disappointed to see me?"

"Never," she said, leaning forward almost into a kiss before pulling away and standing up. "Let's go sit and talk. Okay?"

I agreed, though my heart was clenched with fear at the words that began conversations that never seemed to end well. Maybe it was too late for us after all.

"How have you been?" she asked as we took a seat at a park table. We sat facing each other on the bench seat, straddling it for comfort. As she moved a strand of hair behind her ear repeatedly, I could see her nerves matched mine.

"Pretty good I suppose. Katelyn's finished kindergarten, and she is ready for first grade to start. She turns six this month. She loves school, which is great, but weird. She's grown quite a bit since you've seen her, and she really does want to see you."

"Great, I'd love to see her too. I hate that I missed her when I was in town before. Your mom needed her company a lot more than I did at the time. Since I'll be job searching for the next few weeks, maybe I can spend a few days with her?"

"Absolutely. She'd love it." This was going better than I expected, so I took a chance and reached for her hand. Tensing up, she pulled her hand away. "I'm sorry."

"No, don't be," she said. "There's something you need to know. Disney offered me a full-time position, and I haven't turned it down yet."

"Why not?"

"I need to find a job here first. They've given me a couple more weeks to decide. You understand I need to be able to support myself." I nodded. "For this reason, if you don't want us to be together, I understand. But I wanted to be completely honest with you."

"Hell yes, I want us to be together. I'm going to spend the next few weeks convincing you to stay." No matter what lengths I had to go to, I would convince this woman to stay for good this time.

"We can't tell Katelyn about us."

"You want me to lie to my daughter?" I asked, not fond of the idea.

"Not lie, just don't offer the information of our dating. If she asks you flat out, then you can tell her we are getting to know each other again as friends, which is true."

I pressed my palm against her cheek. "Tell me what we do then."

"Pick me up Friday night for a date? Dinner, movie, maybe a kiss goodnight if you're lucky," she said, throwing me a wink.

"I'm feeling lucky already," I said, grinning back at her.

Friday night finally arrived, and it was time for our first date. After I had knocked twice, Mary Jane opened the door dressed in a low-cut pink dress with baby blue flowers. My eyes drifted over her cleavage, following the curve of her hips, down to her silky smooth legs, and finished at her toes in the sexy heels she was wearing.

Holding her arms out to the side, she spun in a circle, causing her skirt to billow. "Do I look all right?"

My mouth wanted to answer her without words even if it would go against everything that involved going slow. Parts of my body were making it very difficult to stick to my promise.

"No," I said, making her frown. "You look gorgeous."

Biting her bottom lip to hold back her smile, her eyes dipped in embarrassment as her cheeks pinked. Damn, she was sexy. Bending my elbow, I offered it to her. Arm in arm, we walked to the car.

"Where are we going?"

"It's a surprise."

Tapping her foot to the music on the radio, she hummed to the beat as she gazed out the window. At one point, she crossed her legs and her dress slipped down her thigh, exposing almost her entire leg. Wanting to run my hand over her smooth skin, I couldn't take my eyes off her. I swerved and she gasped.

"Are you okay?"

I groaned. "Yeah. Sorry." We pulled into the parking lot of an empty building on Broadway in downtown Nashville. "We're here."

"Um… A Shot in the Dark? If it's a club, I don't think it's open."

"It's not yet, I know the owners." I held my hand out to her, helping her out of the car. "What do you think of the name?"

"It's very cool." Stopping in her tracks, she spun around to face me. "Is this what I think it is?"

Unlocking the door, I held it open and pressed my hand against her back as I eased her inside. "Welcome to our club."

She peered around the room then turned and said, "Gracie told me you were working on this, but I had no idea you were so close to opening. It's beautiful, Derrick."

I stepped behind the counter and brought out a plaque we had made for the foyer of the club. She took it from me and read, "A Shot in the Dark. Owners Ashton, Derrick, and Gavin Collins. Designed by Cameron McIntosh." Setting the plaque down, she wrapped her arms around my neck. "This is amazing." Pressed against me, she bounced excitedly. My hands moved down her sides gradually until I pushed her away slightly.

"Would you like to see the whole place? We're going to open in a few weeks."

"Yes. Show me around!"

Taking her hand, I guided her to the first room. "This will be a singles and party room. We're going to allow it to be reserved for parties and for gatherings such as speed dating nights." Spinning her, I showed her the adjacent room. "This will be the main bar with pool tables, dart boards, and loud music. That's why we have the large doors that can close off the room. It's soundproof so people can converse without screaming."

"Is the music set up yet?" she asked.

"Yeah, why?"

"Dance with me?"

I held up my finger asking for one moment. Running to the back room, I queued up the song "Say Something" by A Great Big World.

With her arms around my neck, mine dropped to her waist. When she placed her head against my chest, I rested mine against hers. Swaying slowly to the words of the emotionally charged song, I breathed in the sweet scents I had missed for so many months.

Our heads lifted and our eyes met. As I traced a finger down her cheek, she closed her eyes, then leaned against my hand. Watching her tongue dart out to wet her lips, I imagined the taste of them. "Tell me if you want me to stop." Slowly, I moved my lips to hers. Before touching them, I asked one more time, "Is this okay?"

Closing the distance between us, her hand pressed against the back of my head, allowing our lips to crash together. Strawberry lip gloss. I hadn't forgotten that taste. Craving more, I wanted to remove her dress and take her right here on the floor where we stood. Soft moans against my lips were too much for me to hold back. When I lifted her up, she gasped and wrapped her legs around me in response. I slipped my tongue into her mouth, then moved her to the booth-style table behind us. Feeling her warmth against my pants, I couldn't stop myself. I slid a hand up her dress and tugged at her panties while she bucked up against my rock-hard cock.

Suddenly, she pushed me back, coming up for air. "Wait, stop."

"I'm sorry." Stepping back, I attempted to catch my breath and adjust myself as the pain of blue balls set in quickly.

Sliding off the table, she adjusted her skirt. "Yeah, because I hated that so much." She winked at me as she delivered the same line I gave her when she kissed me after the funeral. "I love kissing you, Derrick. I love doing a lot of things with you."

A growl issued from my chest. "Damn, sweetheart, you're going to be the death of me, woman."

She giggled, and my pants tightened once more at the sweet sound. When I pressed her into the table, she leaned her head away from me. I dropped my mouth to her neck and let my lips graze her collarbone, then slide up to her ear.

Her palms flat to my chest, she whispered, "If you don't stop, I'll be taking this dress off right here."

"Challenge accepted," I said as I nibbled her ear, then sucked the lobe into my mouth. When I ran my hand up the inside of her leg, she sucked in a deep breath. Then I pulled away from her, leaving her speechless.

"Why did you stop?" she asked breathlessly.

"We're supposed to be taking this slow. If you want me to continue, I will."

"No. I mean, I do, but you're right." She stood up, straightened her dress, and said, "Let's go somewhere more public where we aren't as tempted. Did you have plans past this?"

"I was going to take us to dinner, your choice," I said, truthfully.

We ended up at a place called Brown's Diner. A single-wide trailer made up the front with an attachment on the back for a full restaurant. A bar area filled the trailer while the diner was a mom and pop meat and three establishment.

"I was going to take you somewhere a little fancier," I said, looking around at the low-key restaurant boasting old booths with rips in the seats and neon signs lining the walls.

"Angel, Gracie, and I discovered this place one day. They have the best catfish dinner. They also have home-cooked burgers that are pretty awesome. Give it a shot, you'll love it, and so will your wallet." She smiled, then added, "Plus, it's quiet so we can talk." The waitress came over to take our orders. We both picked something different so we could share. "I want to hear all about the club. Who came up with the name?"

"Gracie. Of course, you can imagine the name Cameron came up with," I said, rolling my eyes.

Tapping her index finger against her chin, she stared up at the ceiling in thought and guessed. "Club Cameron?"

With my index finger, I pointed to my nose then to her. "Tell the lady what she's won, Bob." As she giggled at my game show reference, I took a moment to enjoy the sound of her laughter. "Honestly though, Cameron has been great. His interior design degree came in handy. It was nice to be able to do everything we needed and keep it in the family.

My dad was…." Talking about my dad still choked me up.

Placing her hand over mine, Mary Jane lightly stroked my skin with her thumb. "Your dad helped too?" I nodded, unable to speak until I controlled my emotions. "I think that's great. I'm proud of you. I remember you talking about it being a dream of yours and Ash's. It's really amazing you can make it come true." She paused a moment, then asked, "How's your mom?"

"She's holding up the best she can. There are days I go by to check on her or drop Katelyn off for grandma time, and you can tell she's been crying. They were together over thirty years." Taking a pause, I sip on my glass of water to quell the grief building.

"You know it's been three months, and I still find myself picking up the phone to call him. In fact, I started to call him yesterday to tell him I was taking you out. He loved you, MJ."

Seeing her begin to tear up, I had to look away. "He scolded me for not running after you when you left. He said, 'You don't let a good woman walk out of your life, especially one who is loved by your child. Children don't accept strangers easily, especially into their parents' lives. My Katie is a smart girl and she loves MJ as much as you do.'"

Tears streaked down Mary Jane's face. I reached over and wiped her cheek. "What did I say, sweetheart?"

Swiping the tears away, she tipped her head upward to keep more from spilling forth. "Nothing and everything. It's wonderful to know your father approved of me. It means a lot. You have no idea how much."

Before I could reach for Mary Jane, the waitress arrived with our food. "If it's not too weird, maybe I could spend a day with both your mom and Katelyn?" Mary Jane asked before taking a long sip of her iced tea.

"That's not weird at all. I think my mom would love it. She's very fond of you as well, MJ." My phone rang and I pressed my finger to my lips, asking Mary Jane for silence. "Hey, Katie, are you having fun with Aunt Gracie?"

Katelyn ignored my question and exclaimed, "Aunt Gracie said Mary Jane is back!"

Trying to hold back my grin, I winked at Mary Jane. "Yeah, I did hear something about MJ being back in town. In fact, she asked me if she could spend a few days with you."

Holding the phone away from my ear, you could hear the excited squeal erupting from her. A smile that could light up a room filled Mary Jane's face, and I saw a new glimmer of tears in her eyes. "I need to go, Katie, I'm having a business dinner. I love you."

"Love you too, Daddy."

Less than a minute after I hung up, Mary Jane's phone rang. Laughing, she showed me the caller ID was Gracie, which meant Katelyn. "Hello?" She held a thumb up to me. "Hey, Katie-cat. Tomorrow?" She looked to me for approval. I nodded. "I'd love to spend the day with you tomorrow. Just the two of us. And if it's okay, I'd like to spend a day with you and your grandma when she has a

day free as well… I'll pick you up in the morning then…
Bye." Closing her eyes, she paused and said, "I love you
too, sweetie."

Chapter Seventeen

MARY JANE

Since I'd been home, Derrick and I had been on three dates and I'd spent two afternoons with Katelyn. In between those times, I'd been job searching, sending my résumé out all over town. Time was running out for my decision on the Florida job. They wanted me back by September when the next set of interns came in. My supervisor had called to check in on me the other day and urged me to let him know something soon.

Shortly after talking to the supervisor, I got a call from Katelyn asking me to go to the zoo with her. Nothing could be a better distraction for me than time with her. Nine on the dot, I pulled into Derrick's driveway. As I made my way up the walkway, the front door swung open. Derrick sprinted toward me with a smile on his face.

Dipping me with a long, sensual kiss, he said, "Good morning, beautiful."

Glued to my face was a big dopey grin I couldn't wipe off. "Good morning, yourself." Quickly I pulled away from him before Katelyn saw us.

He laughed and said, "Don't worry, she's still getting ready, that's why I wanted to come steal a kiss before she came out." Grabbing my hand, he led me into the house. At the bottom of the stairs, he called out, "MJ's here, kiddo. Get a move on!"

Katelyn's exasperated voice responded with, "I'm having a bad hair day."

His palm smacked loudly against his forehead; then he turned to me. "What kind of six-year-old worries about bad hair days?"

"The kind who wants to be fabulous of course." Katelyn had her back to me when I came into her room. Her head rested in her hands, her elbows propped up on the vanity as though she was utterly exhausted. "What's wrong Katie-cat?"

She sighed. "I was trying to French braid my hair the way Aunt Gracie taught me, and I can't do it. My arms get too tired."

On the edge of her bed, I took a seat. "Come here, sit between my legs, and I'll fix it up for you. Gracie taught me how to French braid too." Katelyn's hair was almost down to her hips, so it took a few moments for me to braid it all.

When I was tying it off with a pink satin ribbon, Derrick knocked on the bedroom door. "Are you almost done up here, ladies?" He noticed Katelyn's hair and said, "Your hair looks great, boo."

Katelyn ran her hand along the length of the braid. Then she shocked both of us. "Are you two dating again?"

Derrick answered, saving me from embarrassment. "We're getting to know each other again as friends."

Her sweet smile turned into a frown that would break anyone's heart, but especially tore into Derrick and me. We both wanted Katelyn to know the truth but were afraid of hurting her if it didn't work out.

"Are you ready to get our day started?" I asked, changing the subject. Katelyn nodded, and I turned to Derrick. "I'll have her back by dinner."

Derrick reached into his pocket and pulled out his key ring. "Here is a spare key to the house in case I'm not home when you get here. I'm working on some stuff at the club this afternoon."

Adding his key to my set, I avoided eye contact with him. I wanted to kiss him goodbye, to experience the passion we had a few moments ago. At the door, I let my eyes find his and bit my lip at the sexy smirk on his face.

"Great. We'll see you tonight. Text me if you need anything or just to check in." I winked at him because Derrick constantly checked on Katelyn when she was out of his sight. That adorable habit won him more points as a great father, not that there was any doubt.

Our day began at the Nashville Zoo. When I lived in Nashville before, I had a membership; it was my favorite place to go for a walk for exercise or just to enjoy the animals. Instead of buying tickets, I splurged and bought the family level pass so we could come back again later. Listing Derrick and Katelyn as family members, I saw the happy grin on her face.

Our first stop was the meerkat exhibit. Katelyn ran ahead to crawl into the tunnel where you pop up in a plastic tube inside the habitat. With my cell phone ready, I snapped a few pictures of her crawling through, then popping her head up.

Afterward, we went to the petting zoo portion. After an hour there petting every animal in sight, I pulled Katelyn aside. "Hey, kid, it's been over an hour and your dad hasn't called. Can you believe it?" Wrapping my arms around her, we shared a giggle. Together we decided to take a couple selfies to text him.

Pressing our faces together, we gave our best happy smiles. In the second one, we stuck our tongues out and crossed our eyes.

Me: We're proud of you for not checking in for an hour. Thought we'd let you know we're having a blast together. ~MJ and Katie-cat.

Derrick: I promise not to bug you two if you promise to keep sending these pics throughout the day. Deal?

Me: Deal ~MJ and KC

Derrick: KC?

Katelyn rolled her eyes. "Duh."

Me: As in Katie-cat. She said she wanted initials too. ~MJ and KC.

The next text, I omitted the part about me.

Derrick: I love you both. Have fun.

I told Katelyn he said he loved her, but the fact I was included in that made my grin hard to hide. "Let's go have a snack." Katelyn and I stopped in at the park restaurant and bought a basket of fries to share along with a frozen cherry cola for each of us.

Our fries were delivered by the cashier who said, "I love how you did your daughter's hair. It looks so pretty."

Katelyn smiled up at her and said, "Thanks. My mom does the best French braids."

"She certainly does."

Stunned by the girl assuming Katelyn was mine, I was even more thrown by Katelyn calling me mom. What was most surprising was it felt right, and it wasn't scary.

When the woman walked away, Katelyn said, "I've never had anyone to call mom before." An ache in my chest yearned to take away her longing for a mother. "I wish you were my mom," she added before taking a long sip of her frozen drink. Unable to respond, I bit my lip to hold back the tears threatening to fall. Katelyn didn't seem to notice, and then she grabbed her head and exclaimed, "Ugh, brain freeze."

"Take your thumb and press it to the roof of your mouth. It'll make the brain freeze ease quicker." Demonstrating for her, I turned my thumb over and stuck it in my mouth.

She followed my instructions, and a moment later, she felt relief and so did I. I hated seeing her in pain.

"See, you'd be an awesome mom. Dad needs to know

that trick."

Moving around the table, I took the seat next to her. Kissing her cheek, I wrapped my arms around her tightly and said, "I love you, Katie-cat."

She giggled. "I love you too."

"Where do you want to go next? Giraffes? Elephants?"

Tapping her finger against her chin, she rolled her eyes to the side in thought. "Playground?" Almost as excited about playing as she was, I nodded.

Hopping from swings to slides to monkey bars, we finished the day by removing our shoes and jumping in the bounce pit. Collapsing into a pile, we rolled over laughing. At this point, we were both sweating profusely and in desperate need of a shower.

"What do you say we go back to your house for a bit, get cleaned up, and then go out and have a really nice lunch?"

Katelyn held her arms out to me. "Only if you carry me to the car, I'm so tired."

I laughed. "I'm sorry, kid. You want to take a nap before we go out."

She yawned and said, "That'd be nice. You can take one in Daddy's bed."

Derrick's bed, with his sheets carrying his scent was more than I could handle right now. "I think I'll sit on the couch and read for a bit." Because she was walking so slowly back to the car, I stopped and lifted her onto my hip. She rested her head against my shoulder and fell asleep. By the time I got to my car, my arms were killing me. I strapped her in a booster seat in the back and snapped a picture.

Me: I wore her out at the zoo. Taking her back to your house for a nap.

When he texted back, I grinned from ear to ear.

Derrick: Maybe I can come home and join you in that nap? Feel free to take my bed, keep it warm for me.

Thankfully Katelyn couldn't see the big dopey grin on my face right then or she would've wondered what Derrick had said.

Katelyn slept the entire drive home. Carrying her up to her room was quite a chore. I tucked her in before kissing her head and shutting the door as quietly as I could. Since the ride and the struggle to get upstairs didn't wake her, I wasn't sure anything would. While she slept, I ran into Derrick's room and grabbed a quick shower to rub the dirt and grime off myself.

After the shower, I lifted my T-shirt off the counter and sniffed. It smelled terrible, like grass, dirt, and sweat. I knew Derrick wouldn't mind me borrowing one while I threw my clothes in his washer. In his closet, his business suits were hanging, and T-shirts were stacked on a shelf above them. I reached to pull one down and knocked over a shoe box in the process. Pictures spilled out of the box, so I bent to pick them up.

Derrick looked about high school age and had his arms around a girl. Many of the pictures were different poses of him and this girl making faces or kissing. It wasn't as if I thought he'd never dated before, he had a child, but I still felt a twinge of jealousy seeing the photos.

In the next photo, the same girl was sporting a large belly. These were all pictures of Katelyn's mom. Some of the pregnancy pictures make her look really excited. Movie stubs, an ultrasound photo, dried flowers; this was a memory box. Returning the box to its rightful place, I left the closet. It wasn't right for me to go through it, and I should've stopped myself sooner. I curled up on the bed, inhaled the scent of Derrick covering the sheets, and drifted off for a nap of my own.

Feeling the bed sink behind me, strong arms embraced me from behind. Warm lips kissed my cheek, and a husky voice said, "I could get used to coming home and finding you in my clothes and my bed." Feeling his hand against my thigh, I moaned as it glided up to the hem of the T-shirt.

My cheeks flushed with heat as Derrick continued kissing my neck softly; his hands moved inside my shirt, caressing my skin. Before things went too far, I rolled over. "I thought you were kidding about coming home to take a nap." I grinned.

"Only kind of kidding. I had to come home to change into a business suit. I have a meeting this afternoon with an investor for the club." Continuing his journey across my skin, he sucked at the nape of my neck. It would be easy to lose myself in him… to remove the tiny bit of clothing between us and get lost in passion.

Fighting the urge, I sat up. "Do you have a few minutes to talk?"

Joining me, he said, "Of course, what's up?"

"Someone mistook Katelyn for my daughter today, and then she went along with it and called me mom."

Derrick's brow furrowed. "And it upset you?" he asked,

sounding confused.

"No, of course not. I'd love to be her mom, but I'm not." As right as it felt, I couldn't assume the honor was mine to have.

Eyebrows furrowed, he still looked confused. "I know, and so does Katelyn. I don't think I understand the problem. It's not as though I was married to her mom or she died and you're trying to take her place. Her mom's never been in the picture, and that was her choice."

"When I got this T-shirt down, I accidentally knocked over the memory box."

His eyes widened in understanding, and he stood up abruptly. At first I thought I made him mad because he left the room. When he returned, he closed the door and lowered his voice. "Sorry, I wanted to make sure Katie was still asleep and didn't overhear us. That box is an 'I hope she never asks, but I kept this in case she does' box."

Nervous laughter ensued. "That's quite a name for it."

He smirked. "Yeah, sorry. I kept all of that to show Katie she was created out of love. Can you imagine growing up with a mother who didn't want anything to do with you? I don't want Katie to ever feel like she was a mistake. As someone who didn't know me then, how do those pictures look to you?"

"Like two people in love. So much so I was a little jealous at first." Blushing with embarrassment, I dropped my gaze from his.

He grinned. "Oh really?" Then he shook his head to get back on topic. "We thought we were in love back then.

Neither of us knew what it meant though. I despise Katie's mother for walking away and not wanting her, but if Katie wants to know about her, then she will, and she will see good things only. I'll do it for my daughter's self-worth, nothing more. Does that make sense?"

Silently I bobbed my head up and down. He lifted my chin before asking, "What's wrong?"

Fidgeting with my nails and avoiding eye contact, I said, "You amaze me more and more every day."

Interrupted by the sound of his phone ringing, I cursed technology. With a quick glance, he said, "I have to take this. Hold that thought." Excusing himself to the bathroom, he shut the door for privacy. After a few moments, he came out looking stressed.

"Everything all right?"

He ran his fingers through his hair as he scrolled through his contacts. "No. That was the investor I'm supposed to meet with. He can't meet until after seven tonight. I need to see if Ashton or my mom can take Katie overnight in case it runs late. This club is a dream come true for me, but I hardly get to see my girl these days."

I snatched the phone from him. "Do you have any more meetings before that?"

He shook his head "No, but I have to find—"

I covered his mouth. "Let's get something to eat, and then I'll stay with her until you get home."

"Are you sure? I mean, do you not have plans tonight?"

The only plans I wanted to make were with Derrick and Katelyn.

I pulled him in for a quick kiss. "I'm free tonight, and I want more Katie-cat time. We've had a blast today. She needs a quick bath, and while she's washing up, I can dry my shorts. Tonight we can curl up on the couch, watch movies, eat popcorn, and relax. If you'd rather have some time alone with her before then, I can go home for a bit."

Tugging me closer, his breath brushed my lips. "Nothing I'd rather do more than spend time with my two favorite girls for the next few hours."

Kissing my forehead, he pulled away to go wake up Katelyn. As I walked toward her room, I heard her say, "Dad?" in confusion, then cry out, "Oh no! I slept too long and missed my whole day with MJ! I didn't even get to say goodbye."

So much disappointment was in her voice, I couldn't let it continue. "I'm still here, Katie-cat."

Running straight into my arms, she practically knocked me over.

Derrick teasingly asked, "What am I, chopped liver?" Katelyn grinned at him when he winked.

"Your dad had a few hours free and wanted to have a late lunch with us. He has a meeting tonight, so I was going to see if you'd mind me hanging around for a girls' night." Images of a child seeing toys on Christmas morning entered my head as I observed Katelyn's response.

Derrick swiped at her butt playfully. "Go get a bath, kiddo. You smell like the zoo." Pinching his nose with one hand, he used the other to wave in front of it as though trying to push away the stench.

Katelyn stuck her tongue out at him. "What about MJ?"

Derrick stuck his nose against my cheek for a moment and breathed in. "She smells like honeysuckles."

Katelyn pouted. "No fair, she took a shower already." She stomped off to get ready while Derrick pulled me into the hallway.

The moment the door shut, he had me pressed against the wall with his lips brushing against mine as he whispered, "Before I forget to say it, I loved the thought of her calling you mom." With a toe-tingling kiss, he left me standing there in complete awe of him as he went downstairs.

Chapter Eighteen

DERRICK

While Katelyn was getting ready, I had to take a moment
to myself downstairs. Hearing Mary Jane talk about being
Katelyn's mom made me want to scream from the rooftops
with happiness. In a table in the living room, I opened
the small drawer and pulled out a velvet box. The ring I
bought for her, back when we dated before, still sparkled
untouched. It was a princess cut diamond set in a white gold
band. I had bought it the night before she called to end our
relationship. It remained here in a safe place as I kept hope
alive. She wanted to take things slow, and I was just waiting
for the right time.

She called my name, and I shoved the ring back out of
sight before she came in the room. "You ready for dinner?
I'm starving," she said. Katelyn came bounding down the

stairs next.

Our early dinner was pleasant. Originally, we planned to shop for a while after we ate. However, we were only able to eat before I dropped them back off to get to my meeting. Part of me wanted to say to hell with the appointment and spend time with them instead. They were more important to me than anything else. But this club was not only my dream, but it also was for my brothers. As I drove away, they stood waving and blowing kisses. A guy could get used to that kind of home life.

The meeting seemed to drag on forever. The guy wanted every detail of the club down to the brand of toilet paper we planned to buy. When I glanced at my watch, it was after eleven. "Oh my gosh. I had no clue how late it is. I need to get home and relieve the babysitter." Referring to Mary Jane as the babysitter was much easier than referring to her as a woman I was secretly dating… again.

The man snubbed his nose at me. "You want to cut a significant meeting short for a child?"

"*My* child. And yes, nothing is more important than she is. In fact, I'm not sure we want to go the route you do, and this wouldn't be a good investment for you. I'll show you out." I didn't stop pushing him until he was out the door. He stomped away to his car, and under my breath, I muttered, "Yeah, it was a waste of time for me too, buddy. I have a daughter and a beautiful woman waiting for me."

Once I stepped inside the house, I found Mary Jane asleep on the couch. I went to wake her when her phone beeped and flashed. I picked it up and noticed it was a calendar reminder that read: *Two weeks to make a decision about Disney job.* I had two weeks left to convince her to stay with me. I had to take matters into my own hands.

CHAPTER NINETEEN

MARY JANE

A noise woke me from my slumber. I sat up and yawned, realizing it was Derrick. "Hey, you're home. How did your meeting go?"

"I'm sorry it's so late, sweetheart. The guy was a jerk, and it was a complete waste of time. It's after midnight."

Slipping one shoe on, I dreaded the drive home at this time of night. Hoping he'd ask me to stay, I said, "I'll get out of your way."

He grabbed my other shoe and held it hostage. "No way. You can spend the night. We need to talk anyway."

My stomach dropped at the sound of those words. "That's never a good way to start a talk. You're the one who told me that before. Is something wrong?"

He held up my phone, and my breath caught in my throat

as he said, "This flashed on when I came in. You haven't made a decision yet?"

"My job hunt hasn't exactly been successful."

"I hoped you had forgotten to remove the reminder." he remarked.

"I don't know yet." It was impossible to look him in the eyes right now. "I've been putting my résumé in everywhere, and no one has called so far."

"I can make some calls. Why won't you let me help?" His tone oozed with disappointment.

Keeping my composure, I replied, "Because it's something I needed to do on my own. I feel terrible already that I asked Tristan to move here when I can't keep up with my portion of the rent. He can barely afford to take care of himself and Macy on the job he found here. He's still looking for something better, but it could take months."

"Then live with me… with us," he begged. The thought of moving in with Katelyn and Derrick was a dream come true to me. It didn't feel right though to push him into this decision.

"That isn't fair to you."

"I want you with me, MJ. Stay with me, please." Desperation filled his voice as he begged me not to leave.

"Derrick, I don't know. Either choice I make is life altering. I either give you up, my Prince Charming, to pursue a dream career or I give up a dream job to pursue my Prince Charming."

My back was against the arm of the couch as he climbed above me, hovering dangerously close to my lips. With his mouth precariously close to mine, a moan slipped from my lips as I ached for him. Opening my legs, I allowed him to relax against my body. My hands moved up inside his shirt as he pressed harder against me.

"There's no pursuing me. I'm all yours," he growled low against my lips.

I had to push him away. "We can't… Katelyn's upstairs." I squealed as lifted me off the couch and proceeded to carry me upstairs. He went to lock the bedroom door, and I saved him time by dropping my shorts and panties. When he turned around, condom in hand, I was standing in only a T-shirt.

That night he made love to me as though every kiss, every touch was the last. The pleasure he provided was exquisite torture. Nothing would make me forget this moment. I memorized every touch, the feel of his skin touching mine, his moist lips dotting my skin with each delicate taste, and the roughness of his voice when he whispered in my ear. His hair tickled my inner thighs while he ventured below to send me into the throes of passion. Our bodies connected with each thrust, then came together with a groan of release in splendid unity.

When he turned onto his back, I rolled over with my leg thrown over his. He kissed my forehead. "I love you, Mary Jane." When I smiled up at him, he added in a broken whisper, "Please don't leave."

Holding back tears was difficult at this moment. We didn't say another word after his desperate plea. Wrapped up in each other's arms, we drifted off to sleep. In the morning, he slipped out of bed. It was still early, so I jumped up, put on clothes, and followed him.

I heard Derrick's voice as I stepped out of the room. "It was after midnight, pumpkin. That's why I didn't see you before you went to bed."

"You let Mary Jane go home so late?" Katelyn asked.

Before I could turn back to hide in the bedroom, they spotted me standing there.

Katelyn grinned widely and ran over to me in a fit of giggles. "You *are* going to be my mommy!"

Speechless was putting it mildly. All I could stutter was, "What?"

"You came out of my daddy's bedroom. Mommy's and Daddy's sleep in bedrooms together because they love each other. That's what my Uncle Ashton told me. You love my daddy. People that love each other get married, right?"

"I… um…." I stuttered more, and then ran back into the bedroom to change. Words had completely escaped me. The last thing I ever wanted to do was disappoint this little girl.

"Is Mary Jane living with us now?"

"Go get your bath, and we'll talk after."

In the bedroom, I was frantically putting clothes on. The moment Derrick walked in, I defended myself. "I had no idea she was awake. I was going to move to the couch and fix it up as a bed so it would look like I slept there. I'm so sorry, Derrick."

"It's fine, sweetheart."

Stepping forward, he placed his hands on my shoulders to stop me from moving to put on my shoes. "She's right. People who love each other get married. Marry me, MJ."

Chapter Twenty

DERRICK

My proposal didn't go off the way I expected it would. I didn't have a chance to show Mary Jane I had a ring. After proposing, she asked me for a little time to think it over. Not being a *no* kept hope alive for me. I could sacrifice a few days to let her mull it over. No one else even knew we were dating yet. To keep me occupied, I had another meeting about the club. Ashton would be at this one because it was for promoters. We'd made a new decision to have live music nights where we'd have some big names play individual sessions. Ashton was bringing in another promoter friend to extend those contacts even more.

When I walked into the club, they were there chatting. He had Autumn in a carrier strapped to his chest. She was kicking her feet excitedly as they spoke to each other.

Ashton waved me over. "Derrick, this is Grayson."

We shook hands and exchanged pleasantries. Leaning down, I gave the baby a kiss on the head and gave her a few tickles, eliciting adorable baby giggles from her and more feet kicking.

"Where's Gracie this morning?" I asked, wondering why Ashton had their daughter.

"She had classes, and then she's meeting Mary Jane for lunch. Apparently MJ has some important news to tell her. She was kind of vague about it, any idea what that means?" Ashton asked.

"No clue." If she hadn't told anyone about the Disney offer, then telling Gracie she was staying wouldn't be important news, since Gracie wouldn't know Mary Jane had considered leaving. Perhaps it meant she wanted to tell her about my proposal. "Let's get this meeting started. I have to pick up Katelyn in a couple of hours."

If I were to be quizzed on the meeting, I would've failed miserably. All I could think about was what Mary Jane had decided. She said it herself; if she chose the career, she'd be giving up her Prince Charming. She would not intend to come back again. Plus, she knew I couldn't move now and take Katelyn away from her family, especially her grandmother who needed her the most.

On the way to pick up Katelyn from school, a text message came through. Once I pulled over, I checked it.

Mary Jane: I need to see you. Will you be home tonight?

Me: Yes, I'll drop Katie off at Mom's for a while, and

I'll be home by 7?

She sent one more reply.

Mary Jane: I still have your key. I'll let myself in at 6 and make dinner. If that's okay?

Me: Sounds good.

When I picked Katelyn up, she was in one of her happy, talkative moods. I tried to pay attention to everything she said, but my mind was focused on driving and on Mary Jane, and there wasn't room for much else. "Dad!" she exclaimed, exasperated.

"Yeah, boo?" I asked, with no clue what she had been saying.

"I asked you if we could invite Mary Jane to my play at school." She still sounded exasperated that I'd been ignoring her.

"Um… we'll see. Let's go in and see Grandma and talk about it later."

My mom was acting strangely, anxious to get me to leave. It was weird, but I was used to her being weird these days. She probably assumed Mary Jane and I were going to have a romantic night. When I pulled into the driveway, Mary Jane's car was out front.

With candles lit and soft music playing, she waited in the kitchen for me. Dressed in a black wraparound dress tied behind her, she was illuminated by the glow of the small flames. She peered up at me, smiling. "Welcome home."

Chapter Twenty-One 

MARY JANE

My palms were sweating so much I had to keep a dish towel nearby as I prepared dinner. I made Derrick's favorites, which included steak, potatoes, green beans, and rolls. For dessert, we'd enjoy ice cream sundaes. The clock said it was six thirty; each moment that ticked by made me more nervous about the talk we'd have.

Neither of us would ever forget this night, so I wanted to make it as unique as possible. After texting Derrick, I called his mom to ask if she'd mind having Katelyn spend the night. Things could go two ways tonight, either way it would be best not to involve Katelyn.

The sound of a car door alerted me Derrick had arrived. The table was set. I dimmed the lights and lit the candles just as he walked into the kitchen.

"Welcome home," I said as I walked up and gave him a chaste kiss.

"Dinner smells good," he replied emotionless.

"Thanks. How was your day?"

"Let's not do small talk, Mary Jane," he said, sounding exhausted. "You wanted to talk, but I have a few things I need to say first."

Derrick turned his back as he went on his rant without hearing me out. "For the past two years, I've waited patiently for you to finish this internship. And with all the time apart, we still found our way back to each other. My feelings for you never changed. In fact, they've grown stronger. You came to my father's funeral to be with me even though we hadn't seen each other in months. There's no one I could ever love more than you, which is why I proposed. We'll find you a job here eventually, and if I need to, I'll pay your portion with Angel and Tristan because I'll do whatever it takes to wake up with you every morning beside me. And besides all of that, my daughter adores you, and I want you to be my wife, her mother, our best friend. Please don't tell me you're leaving."

While he was turned, I prepared myself for what I was about to say. His words were not ones of anger or blame, but a profession of love and devotion. He wanted me to stay, and I wanted that too.

When he turned around to face me, I was down on one knee with my right hand up in the air holding a gold band.

He stopped, speechless with his mouth open in surprise.

Chapter Twenty-Two

DERRICK

It wasn't my style to beg usually, but this was something I desperately wanted. I couldn't let Mary Jane walk away without a fight. I made that mistake before. It was hard enough to look at the nervousness reflected in her eyes at what she wanted to tell me. Instead of letting her say anything, I began naming every reason why she should stay and every reason why I wanted her to.

When I turned to finally face her, I never expected to see her down on her knee with a ring in her hand. Smiling up at me, she said, "For the last few days, I've gone over all the pros and cons of Orlando versus Nashville. The list is here." She pulled a piece of paper from her cleavage and handed it to me. "As you can see, the pros for leaving are minimal."

When I unfolded the piece of paper, under pros for

leaving it said, "Dream Career." Under the pros for staying it said, "Once in a lifetime love, Prince Charming, the perfect daughter, the life I've always dreamed of" and then listed every one of the people in our lives.

"I'm not sure what rational reason I had for waiting to make this decision since I've loved you and Katelyn from the moment I first met you. I asked your mother's permission to ask for your hand in marriage, and she gave me this."

She held the ring up once more, and I recognized the chain link of the band. "Is that my father's wedding ring?" I asked.

She nodded as tears welled up in her eyes. Trying not to cry, she said, "Derrick Collins, will you marry me?" Before the words were out, the tears were gliding down her cheeks.

I lifted her to a standing position, cradled her face with my palms, and said, "Yes." We shared a brief kiss before I asked teasingly, "Does this mean I have to take your name?"

She laughed, and I lifted her up, then spun her around in a circle. When I sat her down, she said, "There is only one more person I need permission from before we finalize this. I want to ask Katelyn's permission, but I couldn't do that till I had your answer because it wouldn't be fair to you."

The thoughtfulness of her request put a wide grin on my face. "I think that's a great idea. Not that I'm complaining, but what about your job?"

"After your proposal, I called Gavin and he scolded me for not telling him earlier. He contacted a few people, and after an interview, I received an offer. He said it's the least he could do since 'I gave him a freaking child.' His words, not mine." Those sounded more like Cameron's words; those two were starting to meld into one person. We were hoping Gavin wore off more on Cameron than the other way around.

The reality of the moment hit me. I grabbed Mary Jane and bent her over in a passionate heart-stopping kiss. When we came up for air, she giggled softly and asked, "Are you hungry?"

"Not for food."

She winked. "I was hoping you'd say that. I have another surprise for you. I asked your mom to take Katie for the night. She'll bring her by in the morning for breakfast."

"So, we have all night together to celebrate?" I said, excited at the idea. My mind raced with the thoughts of all the things I wanted to do to her tonight. "That's a great surprise."

"Oh, that's not the surprise. Remember the negligee I wore in Atlanta?"

"The white one? Yeah, I'll never forget it." The memory of her in the sheer white lingerie made the room grow hotter.

"Angel bought me the white one for the first time and something else for the second, which I never got to wear." She reached behind her back, untied the sash of her dress, then peeled it open, exposing a red satin and lace bra and panty set that was sheer in more places than there was satin. My eyes drifted to her legs with the red garter belt holding up the black thigh highs with lace tops.

"Have I mentioned I really like Angel?" I asked, unable to tear my eyes away from the sexiest woman to whom I was engaged to be married. She gave a seductive laugh, igniting my lust. I lifted her up onto the counter, pushing the dress off her shoulders to leave her in nothing but the lingerie. "You're so sexy, baby."

My tongue darted out to tickle her earlobe, a move I knew drove her crazy with desire. She locked her legs around my waist and pulled me against her. I felt the heat of her core pressed against my arousal. She tossed her head back and let out a sexy moan as my mouth found her nipple.

We didn't make it to the bedroom. The kitchen counter had never seen action like this before. Her bra fell to the floor, and she began to unlink the garter belt when my hand stopped her. "Leave them on," it came out as a growl. After sliding on a condom, I grabbed her leg and pulled it over my shoulder as I slipped inside her. The fierce passion expressed in her face almost caused me to come undone more quickly than I wanted.

After the counter, I lifted her up, pushed my way through the kitchen door, and moved to the sofa. Sitting on the couch, she straddled me and eased back down over me as her fingers dug into my shoulders with each motion. The couch offered more comfort for us both. Enjoying a slow ride of pleasure, my eyes watched the passion roll across her features; nothing was sexier than the breathy "o" her mouth made.

When we were both spent, we lay on the couch snuggled up together with a blanket thrown over us for warmth. With a gentle kiss to her forehead, I held my hand out with my father's wedding ring on it. "I can't believe my mom gave this up."

"When I told her I was going to propose, she offered it to me. She said your dad hadn't worn it in years because his hands would swell too often. He offered it to Ash when he was getting married, but Ashton told him he couldn't take it because he might want to wear it again one day. Your mom said…."

"It doesn't matter now because he's gone," I guessed, filling in her silence.

"Yes. So, she wanted you to have it."

"Derrick Evans has a nice ring to it," I said humorously, adding her last name to my name.

She smiled. "Oh no you don't. I've been waiting too long to be Mary Jane Collins."

I tipped her chin up to see her beautiful pale green eyes staring back at me. "I've never loved the sound of my last name more than when you said it just then."

Chapter Twenty-Three

MARY JANE

In the morning, I woke up in Derrick's arms, still lying on his sofa. Squinting at the clock on the wall, I realized his mom and Katelyn would be here in less than an hour. I sprang from the couch, taking the blanket with me. When I turned, Derrick was still sound asleep sprawled out in all his naked glory. *Holy smokes, I can't believe I'm marrying this beautiful man.*

"You could take a picture; it'd last longer," he said with his eyes closed but a smirk on his face.

"Oh, this will be etched in my memory forever, trust me." *Lightly tanned skin, muscular thighs, a spattering of dark hair on his chest above a set of washboard abs.*

He opened his eyes, grabbed me around the knees, and pulled me back down on top of him. The look on his face was the happiest I could ever remember seeing on him since we'd met. His smile was contagious as I started to giggle at how giddy he was acting.

"Where were you running off to, Mrs. Soon-to-be Collins?"

"Your mom and Katelyn will be here soon. We have to get showers and start breakfast, and we're running short on time."

"Well, I have a great idea. Let's reduce the water usage with one shower and cut out a few minutes." He suggested, winking at me.

"Race ya," I said, before pushing myself off the couch and running up the stairs. When we reached the bathroom, he grabbed my waist, then pressed me against the wall, capturing my mouth with his in a flaming hot kiss. "If we keep doing this, it isn't going to save us any time," I mumbled against his lips.

After a nice long shower, we dressed, and Derrick went to start breakfast while I cleaned the living room. He pushed through the kitchen door and cleared his throat. "Good thing we got in here before my mom did." In his hands, he had my bra and panties, along with his clothes from the floor of the kitchen where we first made love.

As soon as the words left his mouth, the doorbell rang. "Go! Run those upstairs," I whispered loudly. After one hair check in the mirror, I opened the door.

Katelyn jumped when she saw me. "MJ! I didn't know

you were going to be here." She grabbed me around the waist in a fierce hug. It was hard for me to believe I wanted to give this up.

"Go in and help your daddy with breakfast," I said as Derrick made his way back to the kitchen. "Hi, Mrs. Collins."

She hugged me and said, "It's Maria, sweetheart." Then she whispered, "Don't keep me in suspense. Did you ask already?" Grinning excitedly, I nodded. She covered her mouth, her eyes grew misty, and she said, "Craig would've been so happy at this moment. He'd been rooting for you and Derrick since the beginning."

"I hope Derrick and I are as happy together as long as you and Craig were."

Maria let a tear fall. Her voice cracked as she said, "I hope you get many more years together than we did." She held me tightly when I offered her a comforting hug.

Derrick and Katelyn were in the kitchen whisking eggs to scramble. Katelyn looked up at us and exclaimed, "Daddy's letting me make the eggs."

"Did you put extra shells in mine?" Maria teased.

"Gramma, you don't put the shell in," Katelyn said, rolling her eyes and giggling.

"Do you think you could let your daddy finish those? I want to talk to you a moment." I took Katelyn's hand and led her to the kitchen table. "You know I love you, right?" Katelyn nodded her head in response. "Well, I love your daddy too."

"Are you leaving again?" Katelyn asked sadly.

Brushing her hair back from her face, I said, "No, sweetie. I wanted to ask you if I could stay with you both. I want to be part of your family. I'd like to marry your dad and I want your permission."

Katelyn's eyes grew to the size of saucers. "Really? Will you be my mom?"

"If you'll have me," I said, holding back my emotions with everything I could.

Katelyn threw her arms around my neck, bouncing up and down, squealing. "*Yes!*" Derrick came over and hugged her from behind, sandwiching her between us.

"So, it's official," he said. "We're engaged."

"Daddy, are you going to give Mary Jane her ring too?" Katelyn asked.

"My ring?"

Derrick's look of shock mirrored mine. "How did you know about that?"

"I found it a long time ago in the drawer," Katelyn said with a mischievous grin.

My stomach clenched, but I leaned down and whispered, "It's okay if it's one you bought for someone else. I know she wouldn't understand."

Derrick's gentle smile as he caressed my cheek put me at ease, especially when he said, "Sweetheart, I've never considered proposing to anyone else before. Wait here." A few moments later, he returned with a small square box. "I bought this when we were secretly dating long distance, actually the night before you called me to end things." He opened the box and inside was the most beautiful diamond ring.

"Seriously, you've had it that long?" I ask, with a number

of emotions coursing through me at hearing the news.

"Still have the receipt if you want to see it," he teased.

"I believe you," I said, then started bouncing up and down with my hand out to him. "Put it on me!" I exclaimed giddily. When he slipped it on my finger, it fit perfectly.

An hour after we finished breakfast, we were knocking on Gracie and Ashton's door. The peephole darkened, letting us know someone was standing there. I held my hand up and knew it was Gracie when I heard screeching right before the door was flung open. She grabbed my hand, still squealing excitedly. "We're going to be sisters!"

Next she tackled Derrick in a hug. "It's about time you asked her."

"Actually she asked me," he said.

Gracie flipped around to gape at me. "What?" Derrick held up his hand to show his ring.

Ashton walked up behind me at that moment and said, "Dad's ring looks good on you, bro." Ashton then turned to wrap me in his muscular arms. He kissed my forehead and whispered, "I'm glad you decided to stay." Then louder he said, "It's going to be great having you in the family."

Gracie squealed again while clapping her hands. "We have a wedding to plan," she exclaimed in a singsong voice while bouncing up and down excitedly.

The day had been somewhat surreal, and I needed a moment to gather my thoughts, so I snuck downstairs to their rec room while everyone was bustling around the kitchen making snacks and preparing for a celebration. Once downstairs, I had a moment of clarity and sat down to cry for a moment.

"Mary Jane?" Gavin said as he sat next to me on the couch. "Why are you crying?"

When I glanced up at him, he had baby Addy cradled in his arms, which seemed to round this moment out. "I'm happy. I've had so many crazy good things happen to me in the last two years. I've been lucky enough to have two dreams come true, and I needed a moment to sit and contemplate the impossibility of that for most people. And this little girl," I said, reaching out to caress Addy's cheek, "helped me make your dreams come true. It's been an amazing journey, and there is still so much ahead. It's a bit overwhelming. I was pregnant a couple of months ago, and now I'm going to be a mom to a six-year-old. It's crazy and amazing all at the same time."

"Would you like to hold her? I don't think you have since you were in the hospital. If it's too weird though, I understand."

As I held my arms out, he placed Addy into them. It occurred to me this moment would be difficult, and it was a little hard, but mostly I felt love and protection for her. Seeing how much joy she brought to Cameron and Gavin made it all worth it. Although we shared blood, she didn't feel like mine. I donated an egg and my body in order for her life to be created. She would always be precious to me, but I knew my place in her life.

"I'm your godmother, Addy. You have the two best dads a girl could ever hope for. Don't let Daddy Cam turn you too far to the diva side though. Always be brave like both your daddies. They've been through a lot to get you in their lives. They will protect you with all they have in them. You're the luckiest girl on the planet, more loved than most people will ever know in their entire lives." Bringing her up close to my face, I kissed her soft hair and whispered, "I'll always be here for you, no matter what. I love you."

Gavin wiped the tears falling from his eyes. "Katelyn's a pretty lucky girl to be getting you for a mom. You're a natural, MJ."

"She is a natural for sure," Derrick said as he came down the stairs. "Gavin, Cam needs you upstairs for a moment."

Addison had fallen asleep in my arms at this point. Gavin gave me an awkward look and then looked up the stairs and back. "I can hold her while you go up. We're fine."

Gavin grinned, then kissed Addison's cheek and snuck away upstairs. Derrick took his place on the couch. "Are you all right holding her? Is it difficult for you?"

"Glancing down at her porcelain skin, her chubby cheeks, silky blonde hair, I do see myself in her face, and it stings a little. She's not mine though. I know that. One day I would like to have another one. If you do, of course. It would be nice to have someone to get excited over ultrasounds and kicks with. I experienced that through Cameron and Gavin, but kept myself as distant from it as possible so I didn't become too attached."

Derrick pushed off the couch, leaned over, and pressed his lips to mine. He was careful not to lean too far over the baby while still able to deliver a kiss full of passion. "You're still the most amazing woman I've ever known. To answer your question, yes, I want to have a baby with you one day as well. Finding out about Katelyn was scary, but she ended up being the best thing that ever happened to me. I'd be glad to have four or five babies with you."

I gulped. "Wow… four or five? Let's slow down and start with one."

A soft gurgle slowing turned into a cry and interrupted our conversation. Addison had awoken. I lifted her up to cradle her better, swaying her back and forth with soothing words to calm her. The crying intensified, and I looked up to Derrick for aid.

"Can I try?"

When Derrick took Addison from my arms and cradled her in his strong, muscular ones, it was the most beautiful sight I'd ever seen. She was tiny against his chest as he gently swayed her back to sleep. Addison turned her head and let out one last choked sigh as her sobs extinguished, and she was in dreamland again.

"That gave me a little glimpse of your first year with Katelyn. And I gotta say it kind of made my ovaries explode seeing that side of you." I grinned as he shook his head at my metaphor.

"That would be the first time I made someone's ovaries explode, I believe. I suppose that's a compliment?" he whispered so not to wake the baby.

"Something tells me you've done it before and are unaware. It's the highest compliment these days from a woman." I winked at him.

Chapter Twenty-Four

DERRICK

One Monday afternoon around three, I heard the door shut. "Derrick, we're here!" Gracie called out. When they came into view, I noticed Katelyn sulking on the couch. Before I could ask her what was wrong, Gracie pulled me aside. "She was quiet on the way home. I'm not sure what's up; she wouldn't tell me."

"Thanks, Gracie. I'll call you later when I find out the issue." I kissed her cheek, then walked her out.

Katelyn was still on the couch when I came back in. Taking a seat next to her, I tried to start with our usual talk. "How was your day at school, kiddo?" She shrugged and stuck her bottom lip out. "Did something happen?" She shook her head no. "So, why the sad face?"

She sighed and reached into her backpack, pulling out a

piece of paper. At the top was written "All about my family." Behind the instructions was a slip of paper decorated with flower borders that said, "All About My Mom" and had a list of questions to answer. "This is my homework for the week. I can't do it." She curled up into a ball on the couch with her face buried against the cushion.

I had known this day was coming eventually. Once she started school, I knew it would be difficult to avoid assignments about family that would raise questions and insecurities.

"Sweetie, Mary Jane and I will be married soon. Why don't you answer the questions about her?" I offered.

Frustrated, she cried out, "Look at the questions!" I'd never seen Katelyn so upset before. When I glanced at the questions, I understood further.

"'My mom and I have the same blank.' Is that the question that bothers you?" I asked.

"I don't know if I have my mom's eyes or her hair color. I know I don't match Mary Jane. No one will ever believe she is my mom."

I sighed, then set the paper down and lifted her up onto my hip. "It's time I show you some things."

Once upstairs, I pulled down the box of memories I had kept of her mom. I handed her a picture of me with her mom fully pregnant and smiling. "She looks like Mary Jane. Well, she has blonde hair I mean," Katelyn said, grinning at the picture.

"See. You look like me. Your black hair and blue eyes came from me. Lots of kids look like one parent and not the other."

After looking at a few more pictures, Katelyn seemed to have calmed down. "Thanks, Daddy. Can we keep the box in here in case I want to look again?"

"Absolutely, kiddo. It's here for you anytime you want to see it." Carefully placing the photos back in the box, I put it in the closet once more. "Just ask me, and I'll get them down for you."

She nodded and asked, "Can Mary Jane come over and help me with my homework?"

In less than an hour, Mary Jane showed up. There was a knock on the bedroom door, bringing me out of my thoughts. Mary Jane peered inside. "Hey, can you come downstairs. Katie wants to show you her project."

I smiled and took her hand in mine. "Thanks again for coming over to help her with this. It means a lot to her and to me."

Katelyn was beaming up at me when we stepped into the kitchen. She eagerly handed her paper to me. "Read it out loud, Daddy."

"Okay. My mother's favorite color is blue because it's the color of my eyes. My mother's favorite thing to do with me is have tea parties. I have my mother's eyes and hair color. My mother's name is Derrick, but I call him Daddy." I choked back tears on the last line as I read it out loud. I held it out to Katelyn. "You wrote about me?"

She nodded. "You've been the best mommy and daddy any girl could ever have. I asked Mary Jane if it would be all right to write about you as my mom, and she thought it was a great idea. Do you think so too?"

I wrapped my arms around her waist, lifting her up into a bear hug. "I think it's the best paper I've ever read. I'm honored you wrote it about me." When I set her down, I said, "Now run upstairs and get ready. We're going to go shopping for a little while."

While Katelyn was upstairs, I reached for Mary Jane and pulled her into a passionate embrace, melding our mouths together in one steamy, hot kiss. She pulled away, breathless, and asked, "What was that for?"

"I need a reason to kiss my fiancée?" I asked before leaning in to plant kisses along the neckline of her shirt, tasting inch by inch of her exposed skin.

"No reason needed, and I'm not complaining, that's for sure."

"Thanks for what you did for Katelyn, talking her into doing the report about me."

"I didn't talk her into anything. She said she thought of it after you showed her pictures of her real mom, and she realized she looked exactly like you. She's a very smart girl, that daughter of yours."

CHAPTER TWENTY-FIVE

MARY JANE

I'd spent the day packing up my clothes to take to Derrick's house, which would soon be our house. Tristan and Angel figured out how to work out the bills, and he was happy to be able to have his own room. He swore up and down to me that it didn't bother him to have to work two jobs for a while until he found something better. I promised him I would spend as much time with Macy as I could so she didn't feel lonely.

At first I felt guilty about bringing Tristan and Macy here, but we sat down and had a great talk before I left. Tristan told me she was excelling in school and hadn't been bullied like she had been in Florida. Everything was falling together in the most wonderful way.

Arriving back home, I shut the door behind me and

heard, "I'm in the kitchen." Derrick stood at the stove with his back turned to me. Wrapping my arms around him from behind, I pushed up on my toes to kiss the back of his neck. "Hello, gorgeous," he said, patting my hands that rested against his chest.

"It smells delicious in here."

Turning in my embrace, he faced me to lean down and capture my lips in a kiss. "You smell delicious," he whispered against my ear.

His iPod was playing in the background; he leaned back to turn the music up. Flipping the stove off, he moved me across the kitchen and pulled me close. We swayed to the music, his hands resting against the small of my back, mine around his neck with my head on his shoulder.

"How'd the packing go today?"

"It was fine. My car is full. I thought you might help me bring everything in."

"But of course, that's what I'm here for, right?" Derrick threw me a wink.

Watching him unload the bags, two or three at a time, muscles flexed, was beyond sexy. Once he set them down in the living room, I stepped up behind him, running my hands across his shoulders. "Where's Katelyn?"

"With Ash and Gracie." Turning to face me, he swiped his hand across his forehead, wiping away the sweat. "This isn't everything, is it?"

"Not even close. For now, I was thinking you might want to work up a sweat in a better way." Sliding my hands down his sides, my fingers found their way to his zipper.

His lips turned up in a sexy grin, showing off one dimple. I leaned up for a quick kiss before falling to my knees in front of him.

As my fingers grazed his erection, I felt his cock twitch, and he sucked in his breath. Resting his hands on the couch behind him, he braced himself as my mouth explored the length of him. The salty flavor of precum grazed my tongue.

"Baby, stop," he gasped. He lifted me up. Our mouths crashed together as he frantically unbuttoned my jeans and pushed them to the ground. "Condom," he gasped.

"Don't worry about it. I'm on the pill." Laying me back on the couch, he slid my panties off, quickly tossing them across the room. Wasting no time, he pressed into me. When he rolled me over, I held the couch as he thrust into me from behind, devouring my neck and shoulder blades with his lips as one hand moved around to tease my clit.

"I love you," he whispered in my ear. Rocking me to my core, my orgasm exploded, sending my body into a quiver. Derrick held on, thrusting through my pleasure until he reached his sweet release.

Chapter Twenty-Six

DERRICK

After lying on the couch a few minutes, I remembered we'd have company soon and I needed to finish dinner. Mary Jane helped me in the kitchen until the doorbell rang, and I excused myself to answer it. Tristan stood on the front stoop with his kid sister, Macy, next to him. "Hey, Tristan… Macy. Come in." I waved them into the living room.

Mary Jane came out of the kitchen at that moment and exclaimed, "Macy!" She sprinted to MJ to hug her before they excused themselves upstairs.

"Mary Jane is helping Macy get ready for her first date. I can't believe I'm saying that right now," Tristan said, following me into the kitchen. "She's only my little sister and I'm freaking out about her dating boys. I can't imagine how you're going to feel one day when Katelyn has her first date."

"Sit down," I suggested, motioning to the table.

Tristan eased himself down, looking concerned. "Is something wrong?"

"Tristan, when you two came to my dad's funeral and Mary Jane was eight months pregnant, you went out of your way to convince me to give her a chance to explain. You asked me to give her a chance to tell me in her words what happened. You were already in love with her at that point, weren't you?"

Befuddled, he stumbled over his words. "Um… I, what?"

"I haven't said anything to MJ, but I've seen how you are with her. She cares about you a lot. Because of that, and how worried she's been about you and Macy, I have an offer for you."

Shifting in his chair, he replied, "Look, Derrick, I'm not going to tell her."

"I know. It took a lot of guts to push me toward her instead of leaving things be or trying to come between us. You're an honorable guy, T. I can see that through the time we've known each other and through the way you look at MJ. I knew you cared about her, but I didn't know the full extent. Thank you for respecting what we have. It means a lot to me." In a show of sincerity, I extended my hand to him, and he shook it without hesitation. "MJ said you were having trouble affording the rent where you and Angel are now that she's moving out."

"I'm looking for a better paying job. It's not a big deal. We can make it work for a little bit." Tristan seemed embarrassed I brought the matter up; it was easy to see it hurt his pride to not be able to take care of Macy the way he needed.

"That's where I'd like to help. I'd like to hire you as a bartender for my club. Between what we'll pay hourly and the tips you'll earn, you should find it pays much better than your current job."

Tristan considered the offer for a moment before saying, "That sounds perfect. The only problem is I don't know much about being a bartender. I know how to make a few drinks and how to pour beer without too much foam, but that's the extent of my knowledge."

"There's a bartender school we can send you to. The course takes about two weeks, which is perfect because the club doesn't open for another month. We'll cover the cost. All you have to do is agree to work with us for a year, and it will be no cost to you. That's the offer we'd decided on for any bartender, so this isn't special treatment because you're a friend.

"I would like you to be head bartender. You'd be over the other two, possibly three, we would hire. MJ also told me you've been a supervisor in the past. So, tell me what you think."

Tristan seemed overwhelmed at the offer I'd presented to him, so I sat back and waited for his answer. After a few moments of silence, he replied, "I'll take it."

"Great! I'll get you set up for classes as soon as possible. And during the next couple of weeks, I'll want you to sit in on the hiring with Ashton and me if that's all right with you."

"Sounds great. Look, Derrick, I appreciate this opportunity. It's going to mean a lot to Macy too."

Mary Jane poked her head into the kitchen and asked, "Tristan, Macy's ready. Can you guys come out here and see what you think?"

Tristan nervously walked into the living room, and his mouth dropped open at seeing his little sister all dressed up. She was only fourteen, and Mary Jane dressed her appropriately for her age in a lavender dress that fell just below her knees. She had curled her short hair and clipped a flower on the left side to pull it back.

"You look beautiful, Macy," I said as Tristan stared, completely speechless.

"Thanks, Derrick. Tristan, do I look all right?"

Tristan bent to hug her and said, "You look gorgeous, Macy. Thanks, MJ. I'll call you later and let you know how her date goes."

Chapter Twenty-Seven

MARY JANE

The opening of A Shot in the Dark had finally arrived. For the past month, I'd barely seen Derrick due to all the last-minute details they had to complete. Gracie and I were in charge of putting together the invites for opening night. The evening was for a limited amount of people. We sent out invitations, but we'd also arranged for radio stations to give away a number of special passes to the public as well. Once those were given out, we'd also allow the first fifty people who showed inside.

Tristan and I hadn't spoken since he called me to tell me Macy's date went perfectly. He said the boy she went out with was a perfect gentleman. He dropped them off at the restaurant and then managed to be seated in view of them without being noticed. He said he'd never seen Macy smile so much in the last few years. After that day, he'd been busy with bartending school and helping Derrick and Ashton interview the other potentials.

Gracie and I had designed the theme for the night around the rock band Ashton had scheduled. We'd set up several contests for people to win different gift cards and a grand prize of two free drinks for a year for every night they came to the bar. Gracie had come up with a great game to go with the name of the bar. There'd be a lineup of three shots and the person would be blindfolded as they were poured. Then they'd have to guess what was in each shot. Whoever named them all first would win the prize associated with that game.

We'd even arranged business with a company offering sober rides. Everything was coming together perfectly. Ashton, Derrick, Gavin, and Cameron were at the bar putting the final touches on before the club opened. Gracie and I gathered up Autumn, Katelyn, Addison, and Macy to go over to Maria's for the night. We'd offered to pay Macy to help Maria with the other three, and she was more than willing.

The doorbell rang, and I ran downstairs knowing it was Angel and Gracie coming over to get ready. They paraded in with garment bags and a box of makeup. "Let's get you ladies looking hot for your men's big opening night!" Angel exclaimed.

"This is so unreal to me right now," Gracie said. "Ashton and Derrick have been talking about running a club for so long it seemed like a dream was all it would be. I'm so proud of them both."

"Me too," I said. "It's so great they were able to put it together as a family."

"All right, enough reminiscing, ladies. We only have a couple of hours. Let's figure out which of these dresses you're wearing so we can take the others back tomorrow."

Angel worked at a dress store in Green Hills. Her boss was a childhood friend of her mom's, so she let Angel get away with anything she wanted. For this weekend, she allowed her to gather an abundance of dresses in our sizes so we could pick the perfect one for tonight.

It took us over an hour to settle on each of our dresses for the evening. Gracie chose a crimson, strapless, knee-length dress with a black lace overlay and black velvet belt that cinched the waist. She paired this with the black cowboy boots with red stitching Ashton bought her one night when they were out and her heel broke. They were sentimental to their relationship, so she was ecstatic Angel found a dress to match them.

Angel chose a maroon, sleeveless dress that hugged her curves and accented her olive skin tone perfectly. Mine was a strapless, beaded, pink and black tulle cocktail dress. The dress was mostly black with sparkles covering the tulle material. A large pink satin bow was around the waist, and a single strap of pink satin roses traveled over my left shoulder.

Once the three of us were ready to go, we piled into Angel's car for the evening. She drove because Gracie and I would both ride home with our guys at the end of the night.

The party had already started when we arrived.

Photographers were outside taking pictures of the building and the crowd waiting to get in. It looked like a scene from the red carpet, something I'd only seen on television.

The bouncer stood at the door checking a guest list. Gracie sauntered up to him. "Hey, Bobby." She grinned. He leaned down to hug her and give her a kiss on the cheek. "Hey, Gracie, it's great to see you again, especially when you aren't kicking and screaming over Ash's shoulder."

Gracie laughed and blushed at the memory Bobby brought up. He'd been a bouncer at a club they attended one night. Ashton kept his promise to Bobby. He'd found him a boss who wasn't homophobic. Once they'd decided on when the club would open, Bobby was the first one Ashton called.

"Ladies, you all look drop-dead gorgeous," Bobby said as he opened the rope gate to let us through.

"Thanks, Bobby," we all chimed in as we stepped passed him.

The first one we spotted was Tristan at the bar. He gave us all a wink and a thumbs-up. Gracie spotted Ashton, so she ran over to greet him. I watched as he noticed her boots and grinned before dipping her in an adoring kiss.

Angel moved to the bar and began to flirt with Tristan while I searched desperately for Derrick. A hot breath against my ear said, "You are the most beautiful woman in this entire room, hands down."

Turning around, I came face to face with the sexiest man I'd ever known, Derrick. His smile made me want to push him into the back room and have my way with him right then. His hand took mine and spun me around in a circle.

"What do you think?" I asked.

"I stand by what I said. This dress looks great on you." He pulled me close and whispered, "I bet it'll look even better off."

"You'll have to wait until later to find out."

"Dance with me?"

The dance floor was full of couples slow dancing to the song being played on stage. "I'm so proud of you. This place is amazing, Derrick."

"I couldn't have done it without my brothers. It's still so hard to believe how it all came together. I brought Katelyn here last night to show her what it looked like. She was so excited. She asked if she could have her next birthday party here."

Laughing, I said, "I guess if we did it during the day and had it in a private room where we could lock the bar it wouldn't be too bad."

"I love you, Mary Jane. I couldn't have done this without you either, you know that?"

"I love you, Derrick."

He twirled me around, then spun me back into his arms with my back against his chest so I could see the rest of the room. He nuzzled his head against my cheek and said, "Did you notice the paintings around the room? They're all Ashton's, and they all depict an event from each of our lives. The one with the couple standing under the stars describes his life with Gracie. See that one." He pointed to a painting to our right. "The two men standing, cradling a baby with a pale rainbow in the background signifies Cameron and Gavin with their struggles and dreams. Last but not least, this one." He spun me around to see the wall behind us. "The blonde woman on the beach walking toward the man standing in the city with a rose… it represents our journey to each other."

The amount of time and thought that went into these paintings was unbelievable. Gracie had shown me Ashton's work before, but it had never touched me the way it did at that moment. It left me filled with hope and love but no words.

Everything was perfect. The club, the rings on our fingers symbolizing our future, Katelyn becoming my daughter, I couldn't dream up a better moment. A career at Disney had been my dream once upon a time, but dreams changed as we grew older. I was living my dream, and I wouldn't want to change a thing about it. For the rest of the evening, we danced to every song until the crowd died down and the only people left were our friends and us.

Occupying one of the empty booths, the girls slipped off their heels and dropped them next to the table. Ashton grabbed us a round of drinks and sent the bartenders home for the night.

Raising my bottle of beer in the air, I said, "A toast to a successful opening night."

After a drink, Ashton raised his next. "A toast to the happy couple. And to a woman I'll be proud to call my sister-in-law."

Cheers, glasses tinkling, and laughter filled the nightclub for the next few hours as we all celebrated the Collins brothers' success.

# Chapter Twenty-Eight

MARY JANE

The evening for the play at Katelyn's school arrived. For music class, the children were putting on a performance of *The Little Mermaid*. Katelyn was excited to be playing Ariel. We'd been working on her costume for weeks. Maria had sewn a beautiful teal mermaid tail for her with shimmering clear fins at the bottom. I put together a seashell bra that I attached to a flesh-colored leotard. We'd ordered a wig from a costume shop in Nashville known to be the best place to get authentic cosplay outfits. The wig fitted Katelyn perfectly, so much so that she wanted to wear it all the time.

"Katie-cat, it's time to go. You ready for your play?" She had her back to me, adjusting the vibrant red wig with her hands before turning to show me her face. "Oh… you did your makeup." I tried to not show too much shock at the glow on her face from the red lipstick to the circles of rosy pink blush.

Exasperated, she said, "I should've waited on you. Will you help me redo it?"

"We don't have to redo it. Let's just tone it down a bit to let your natural beauty through." Using a cotton ball, I removed enough of the pink blush to give her cheeks a subtle tinge of pink. She had chosen navy blue eye shadow, which I removed entirely and replaced with a pale blue color that we added a soft white sparkle on top. Her red lips were perfect to stand out for the play. "How's that?" I asked, turning her to look in the mirror at the finished product.

Her eyes lit up with excitement. "Perfect!" She turned to hug me. "Thanks, Mary Jane." We ran downstairs to find Derrick patiently waiting for us.

His broad smile as his eyes fell upon Katelyn told me he was impressed with the transformation as well. "You look beautiful, boo." On the way to the school, Derrick let Katelyn listen to her iPod to practice the songs. We could hear a whisper of her singing along, but it kept her from hearing what we talked about.

Derrick took my hand in his, bringing it to rest on his thigh. "Lanie will be there. The play is being put on by kindergarten through second graders. I wanted to make sure you knew so you weren't surprised."

"Don't worry about it, Derrick. I'll be fine. You guys only went out twice, and I can't blame her for being a little catty when she met me. I'd fight for your attention too if I were her."

At the school, we spotted Gracie and Ashton's car with an open space next to it, so we parked beside them. Derrick loaded himself down with the costume bags and camera while I escorted Katelyn to the dressing room they'd set up in the music classroom. Lanie was standing at the doorway to greet us. Derrick walked in first, and she greeted him normally, and then her face grew shocked as she laid eyes on me. She dropped her gaze and awkwardly greeted me before telling Katelyn she looked amazing and would do great.

While Derrick helped Katelyn into her costume, I stepped over to Lanie. "Hi, we haven't officially met. I'm Mary Jane."

Lanie smiled. "I owe you an apology. I was quite rude to you at Derrick's father's funeral."

I waved my hand to stop her. "Let's not worry about that now. As far as I'm concerned, this is our first meeting and it's going well."

She seemed relieved at my ease with her. Perhaps she was expecting a dramatic moment with a woman taking a stand for her man. That wasn't my style though. Derrick wanted me. I didn't need to claim my territory or act like a jealous woman to keep him around.

"Congratulations, by the way. Katelyn told me she's getting a mom, and I see by the beautiful ring that it's you." Lanie's face expressed that she was sincere, and I realized she wasn't the catty woman she had appeared to be.

"Thank you."

Derrick and I wished Katelyn luck before slipping out to

find our seats. Gracie and Ashton were waiting in the front row, waving at us excitedly. Autumn bounced on Ashton's knee. Before we sat, I bent to greet Autumn with a smile and to tickle her adorable chubby tummy. She giggled and flashed me a two-tooth grin, making me laugh. The lights dimmed, Derrick took the seat next to Ash, and I sat next to Derrick. When the first scene started, the mermaids were all singing about their little sister's debut before they realized she wasn't there.

When Katelyn appeared for the next scene, she started to sing her lines very softly. She stopped for a moment, glancing around at all the people staring back at her.

Patting Derrick's leg, I whispered, "I'll be right back." Entering the stage door to the left, I stood out of sight and motioned to Katelyn to get her attention. She was on the brink of tears. When I began to softly sing the words to the song for her, she turned to face the crowd again and sang with me. At the end of the song, she seemed to have lost her fear, but I stayed next to the stage in case she needed me.

When the play was over, the kids were given a standing ovation by all the parents while Derrick hooted in the front row for his daughter. Katelyn tugged on Lanie and whispered something. Lanie nodded and turned to the crowd. "Katelyn would like you to give a round of applause to her mother, Mary Jane." She turned to face me, waving me forward. Holding back tears, I stepped out and walked to take a bow. Katelyn beamed from ear to ear. When I knelt down, she ran into my arms to hug me. We turned to take a bow together and my eyes met Derrick's. He stood there with his hand to his mouth still calling out cheers louder than anyone.

When we stepped off stage, he presented Katelyn with a dozen roses, from which she pulled one out for me and said, "Thanks for saving me up there." She peered over at Derrick and motioned him to her level. She whispered something in his ear.

With a smile on his face that could light up a room, he briefly glanced at me and said, "I think she'd like that a lot."

Katelyn wrapped her arms around me and said, "I love you… Mom." And that was all I needed to know I made the best decision of my life by choosing this love. Not only did I gain Prince Charming, but my very own princess to raise as well.

CHAPTER TWENTY-NINE  

DERRICK

Two weeks after my sixteenth birthday, I got a call that no teenage boy wanted to get. My girlfriend, of a little over a year, was crying on the phone because the stick had turned pink. I had no idea what stick she was even referring to until she finally screamed out she was pregnant. At that moment, I thought my life was over. My head was spinning, I felt sick to my stomach, and I was sure my parents were going to kick me out of the house. Instead, my parents sat me down and talked to me about being responsible and then continued to support me every step of the way, even when I made the decision to raise this child on my own. Terrified did not describe what I felt when I first held Katelyn in my arms.

Six months after proposing, I married Mary Jane in a

small ceremony in the park where we first met. Ashton stood beside me as my best man with Katelyn next to Mary Jane as her maid of honor. We wrote our own vows, pledging to never let anything come between us again.

On our wedding night, Mary Jane had promised me a gift. The only hints she gave was that it wasn't something I could unwrap, but it would give me a lifetime of happiness. After we had consummated our marriage officially, we were lying there in bed when I remembered the present. "So, where's my gift?" I teased.

With a mischievous grin, she reached for my hand and slid it under the sheets. At first I thought she was trying to be naughty, until she placed my palm against her stomach.

"Sorry, you're going to have to wait another eight months to see it."

The fear, the devastation, and utter turmoil I felt at hearing I'd be a dad the first time wasn't there this time. Katelyn's entire life passed before my eyes as I took in the news I'd get to do it all over again, and this time I couldn't wait. We'd had the talk about kids, to the point Mary Jane stopped taking birth control two months ago. The doctor told us it wasn't likely we'd get pregnant right away, so the news came as a pleasant surprise.

Thinking ahead, she scheduled her ultrasound for the day after our wedding so we could see the baby together. Seeing our baby on the screen made everything come together so perfectly. Being a dad had been the thing I was most proud of in life, and I was getting to do it all over again.

We had spent our wedding night enjoying a suite at a

local ritzy hotel our friends had paid for as a wedding gift. Tristan and Angel kept Katelyn for us so Ashton and Gracie could have a break too since they'd had her a lot during the wedding plans. Mary Jane hadn't told anyone about the baby. She wanted me to be the first to know, and then Katelyn.

So as soon as we arrived at Angel and Tristan's house, we asked them to leave us alone for a moment.

Mary Jane pulled the ultrasound photo out of her purse and slid it across the table. "Do you know what this is?"

Katelyn stared at it and said, "It looks like the picture Aunt Gracie showed me of Autumn when she was in her belly."

Mary Jane's grin widened. "That's right. It is like that, but not the same picture."

Katelyn looked up at me, then over to Mary Jane. "Are we having a baby?" she asked, innocently including herself into the mixture, which I thought was great.

"Yep, we are!" Mary Jane exclaimed.

Katelyn squealed, then ran to hug both of us. "Is it a boy or girl?" she asked.

"We won't know that for a little while. All we know is you're going to be the best big sister ever, right?"

She rolled her eyes. "Gee, no pressure."

We'd asked Tristan to call the rest of the family over so we could relay the news to them all at once. They were all bouncing in their seats. We were pretty sure they'd figured out the news, so we decided to throw them off a bit. "We're moving to Florida for MJ to work for Disney. She's received an incredible offer, and after careful consideration, we've decided it's the best choice for our family."

Their faces went from excited to heartbroken in seconds. A resounding "What?" erupted from all of them at once.

Mary Jane and I both laughed and said, "Gotcha!" She held up the ultrasound picture and the relief in the room was tangible. After a few uttered curse words, cheers of excitement and joy filled the room.

Standing back from the celebration, I took in my family. We were a diverse group of people. We'd made mistakes, we'd loved, lost, and loved again, and we were still standing after everything that had been thrown at us.

A couple of clichés were definitely real in my life. One was that everything happened for a reason. If I hadn't become a father, I wouldn't have needed a babysitter the day Ashton was in an accident, and I wouldn't have met Mary Jane. And two, sometimes when you love someone you had to let them go, and if they were truly yours, they'd come back. Giving Mary Jane up was one of the hardest things I'd done, but it paid off when she stepped back into my life. We'd been on the same path all along. By following the curves in the road, we ended up right where we wanted to be in the first place.

THE END

ACKNOWLEDGEMENTS

First and most importantly, I must always thank my number one guy, the man who gives me writing time every night, the one who has been my muse when I need advice on a funny line or direction on how a man thinks. Daniel, my husband of almost twelve years, has supported me through this entire journey, never once suggesting I give up or stop writing. He accompanies me to every event, grounding me when my anxiety goes into full effect. He's my rock and my strongest supporter. Without him, I'd have never taken the first step toward writing.

Secondly, my mom. She has read every book I've written. She "pimps" me out to her friends, family, her swim group, and anyone else she can think of. Both of my parents have supported me by attending signings, donating prizes for readers, or just offering a cheering applause when I have news on a new book.

To the amazing ladies of Hot Tree Publishing, thank you for believing in my writing and taking the time to help make my books reach more readers. To Becky for all the words of wisdom, and amazing support. To everyone who has worked on the edits of this book, especially Peggy who gave me such amazing feedback and helped me turn a story around to make it even better.

Last but not least, thank you to all the readers who have been with me since the beginning, the new readers who are just now discovering my work and e-mailing or messaging me to let me know how they enjoy them. Thank you to anyone who has ever written a review. Whether good or bad, you've helped me grow as a writer and given me more confidence to continue this journey.

ABOUT THE PUBLISHER

Hot Tree Publishing opened its doors in 2015 with an aspiration to bring quality fiction to the world of readers. With the initial focus on romance and a wide spread of romance sub-genres, we envision opening up to alternative genres in the near future.

Firmly seated in the industry as a leading editing provider to independent authors and small publishing houses, Hot Tree Publishing is the sister company to Hot Tree Editing, founded in 2012. Having established in-house editing and promotions, plus having a well-respected market presence, Hot Tree Publishing endeavors to be a leader in bringing quality stories to the world of readers.

Interested in discovering more amazing reads brought to you by Hot Tree Publishing or perhaps you're interested in submitting a manuscript and joining the HTPubs family? Either way, head over to the website for information:

WWW.HOTTREEPUBLISHING.COM